THE RESISTERS

o   o   o

ERIC NYLUND

RANDOM HOUSE  NEW YORK

Visit us on the Web! www.randomhouse.com/kids

Educators and librarians, for a variety of teaching tools, visit us at
www.randomhouse.com/teachers

Library of Congress Cataloging-in-Publication Data
Nylund, Eric S.
The Resisters / Eric Nylund. — 1st ed.
p. cm.
Summary: When twelve-year-olds Madison and Felix kidnap him,
Ethan learns that the Earth has been taken over by aliens and that
all the adults in the world are under mind control.
ISBN 978-0-375-86856-6 (trade) — ISBN 978-0-375-96856-3 (lib. bdg.) —
ISBN 978-0-375-89926-3 (ebook)
[1. Science fiction.   2. Extraterrestrial beings—Fiction.   3. Brainwashing—Fiction.]
I. Title.
PZ7.N9948 Re 2011   [Fic]—dc22   2010019230

Printed in the United States of America

10 9 8 7 6 5 4 3 2 1

First Edition

For Kai,
with all the love a father can give—
this story is for you.

° ° ° CONTENTS ° ° °

THE LAST TIME FOR ORDINARY

ETHAN BLACKWOOD PREPARED FOR BATTLE.

In the months to come, Ethan would look back and marvel that there could be a fight in which someone *didn't* get hurt ... or his life or the entire human race wasn't constantly at risk.

At the time, though, he did think of it as a battle. No one *ever* thought of it as a game—not when you strapped on six hundred pounds of nuclear-powered exoskeleton athletic suit.

Inside his suit, he crouched on the sidelines of the Northside Elementary athletic field. Ethan and his teammates huddled around Coach, listening to his plan. Each of them wore an external frame that was stainless steel and hydraulics and orange gecko-grip-soled feet ... except, of course, Coach. He wasn't in a suit. For now, he was half their size, a dwarf among giants.

It was all "defensive action" this and "special team maneuver" that.

Really, all the fancy terms came down to setting up one last play.

This was a special repair time-out before the last seven seconds of the state semifinal soccer championship: the Grizzlies vs. the Westside Warriors. The score was tied.

Twelve-year-old Ethan was captain of the Grizzlies. It was a crushing responsibility for a seventh grader surrounded by the eighth graders on his team.

But Ethan *thrived* under pressure. The tougher the midterm, the more he crammed. The tighter the spot in a match, the more Ethan moved like a cat in his suit— twisting around defenders—even making those near-half-field five-hundred-foot kicks!

Inside the formfitting cockpit, sweat dripped off the end of Ethan's nose.

There were a few moments in Ethan Blackwood's life that had burned themselves into his memory: a splinter that'd gone *through* his hand when he was four (his mom had pulled it out); winning two blue ribbons at school science fairs—one for the biology of the nerve, another for a robotic arm; last week at the Sadie Hawkins dance, when he'd fumbled for Mary Vincent's hand (although technically *she* had taken *his* hand)—and this moment.

Like when he'd had that splinter, won the science fairs, and held Mary's hand—Ethan felt burning, churning flutters deep in his stomach.

But this was different. It wasn't just about Ethan. His whole team had a stake in this, and that made it vital that Ethan get it right. "Blackwood!" Coach Norman said. "Your head in this match?"

Ethan Blackwood looked at his teammates. The snarling-bear emblems on their chest plates stared back at him; the pressure circuits in their arms and legs twitched and hissed as if the suits were somehow nervous too.

Ethan met the dark gray eyes of Coach. "Yes, sir."

Coach went on then . . . something about the importance of focus . . . as Ethan's gaze drifted past him, along the sidelines of the field and the bleachers.

The cheers were completely distracting.

Ethan adjusted the filters on his targeting camera to shade the huge lights overhead that turned night into day on the field. He spotted his mom in the stands, with her golden Filipino features smiling, and Dad, with his strong Cherokee jaw clenched (Ethan had inherited the same quick smile, and the same quick-to-frown jawline). They'd be proud of him win or lose. Even his brother and sisters had come tonight: little Dana and Danny, still in diapers, and his older sister, Emma, who gave Ethan a thumbs-up.

Something was out of place, though.

Sitting a row up from his family were two strangers.

Ethan knew everyone at school and most of the opposing Westside Warrior fans, but these two students, a guy and a girl, he'd never seen before.

They weren't in Northside's red and brown colors or

Westside's green. Even though it was prohibited by the school's dress code, they wore jeans and black T-shirts. The dark colors set off their superpale skin.

The boy took up space for two people in the stands—not "fat" big, but more like a weightlifter. His T-shirt looked two sizes too small and about to rip. His head was shaved, showing only a faint shadow of stubble.

The girl was thin, and she seemed to drown in her oversized T-shirt. Her blond hair stuck up in a spiky ponytail.

Something else set them apart. The look in their eyes was the strangest thing. Pure tension—like this was a life-or-death situation.

Well, how could anyone *not* be fascinated by soccer? Especially *this* match! But these two scrutinized everyone on the field . . . as if they weren't interested in the game, exactly, but were looking for someone.

Coach Norman finished his final instructions (which Ethan realized he had completely blanked on) and shouted, "Break!"

Ethan instantly forgot the two strangers and snapped his head back into the match.

His teammates placed their hands in the center of the huddle with machine-like precision, raised them in salute, and shouted, "*Grrrrrrrrrizzlies!!*"

Ethan and his team then turned to face the Westside Warriors.

Ethan should have asked about Coach's instructions,

but his parents had always told him to go with his gut when in doubt.

That was what he'd do now.

He whispered to his fellow striker, Bobby, "Give me three Mississippis and then pass me the ball."

Bobby looked back at Coach, whose word was law. But Bobby also knew when Ethan Blackwood was in the zone . . . and when Ethan couldn't fail to make a shot. He nodded.

The referee let loose a blast from his whistle—a steam-powered trill that gave Ethan a jolt every time he heard it.

Bobby tossed the soccer ball at Ethan from the sidelines.

Two green-clad Warriors bounded toward Ethan, twelve hundred pounds total of gleaming metal pistoning at him like freight trains.

Ethan's heart hammered. He kicked the ball back to Bobby and counted.

One Mississippi. Ethan sprinted at forty-five miles per hour to the midfield line.

Two defenders covered Bobby.

Two Mississippi. Ethan dodged. The single defender on him overshot his position, lost his balance (even with his gyros on max), and landed in a heap with a tremendous clatter.

Three Mississippi. Among the *squicks* of soles on the green-painted metal field, there was the unmistakable *whoosh* of an incoming, solid-rubber, high-velocity ball.

Ethan stomped and spun.

For a fraction of a heartbeat he saw the ball he knew Bobby would pass—a blur rocketing at two hundred miles an hour—right to him.

Ethan head-butted the ball downfield and sprinted after it.

The crowd screamed—but the sound faded . . . drowned by Ethan's thundering pulse and the thumping of his suit's hydraulics.

Three Warrior defenders raced after him.

Ethan twisted, gears and gyros screaming in overdrive as he caught up to the ball and dribbled it between his feet.

Warriors closed on all sides to block him. There was no more time.

He had to take the shot now—still three hundred feet from the goal.

He snapped on his suit's targeting system. Arrows and grid lines popped onto his view screen.

The goalkeeper faced him, and suddenly Ethan's screen fuzzed with static.

He was getting jammed by the goalie!

Less than two seconds on the clock.

Ethan crouched, tensed the frame of his suit—head to boots—and kicked the ball as hard as he could.

The ball ripped through the air, a smear of black and white.

It bounced once and shot off at a different angle because of the wicked spin he'd given the ball.

The goalkeeper tried to reverse his direction to catch it.

But the ball screamed past his fingertips—

—and into the net, stretching it to the tearing point, and then dropping to the ground, smoking from the incredible air friction. It rolled to a stop.

The end-match buzzer sounded.

Ethan stood stunned, not sure he'd seen that right.

His team surrounded him, clapping Ethan on the back with metallic clangs, hugging him, and even Coach Norman shook his head with disbelief and smiled. The team lifted Ethan up on their shoulders.

Despite his suit, Ethan felt light as a feather—like he could fly.

Everyone in the Grizzlies section of the bleachers ran onto the field, waving red flags and cheering.

They'd won! The Grizzlies were going to state finals!

It was like he'd won every science fair *and* just taken Mary Vincent's hand.

But some instinct nagged Ethan. He felt uneasy and glanced up at the bleachers.

The only people still there were the two strangers.

The pale boy and girl stared at him. The girl made a chopping motion to her friend—and they stalked off.

Goose bumps crawled down Ethan's back.

ABDUCTED

ETHAN SHOWERED OFF HIS SWEAT AND THE suit's grease and gear grime. He'd whooped it up and enjoyed more back slaps and high fives from his teammates in the locker room. But then they'd all gone off to some celebration party.

Ethan had told them to call him later and he'd catch up.

He wanted to walk home alone. He needed a few minutes to get used to his own body, minus the six hundred pounds of exoskeleton.

Really, he wanted time to think. So much had happened so fast.

He toweled dry, got dressed, and marched off campus onto the streets of Santa Blanca.

He knew every inch of his neighborhood. He spied imprints in the sidewalk's concrete of tiny hands and scratchy initials made by him and his sister Emma. He inhaled, smelling freshly cut lawns, barbecuing hamburgers, and a cool breeze from the mountains that surrounded his town. Streetlamps cast circles of light, but between them it was a clear, moonless night, brimming with stars.

He took it all in because it might end in a year. That's when he'd be tested and, hopefully, certified mentally, physically, and socially ready for high school.

That's when he'd leave the neighborhood.

Not everyone got tested at the same time. You had to be mature enough and have the grades and the right combination of extracurricular activities. It was a *big* deal— maybe the most important thing that would ever happen to Ethan.

Part of him *never* wanted to leave.

His family was here. He knew every person here and every book in the library. It was familiar, comforting, and safe.

But another part of him wanted to see the world. Do things you couldn't do in the sleepy community of Santa Blanca.

Winning the match tonight had been great. So would be going to the state championship. If they won *that*, Ethan and his teammates would get scholarships to the high school of their choice.

It would be MIT Prep for him, of course, the best science high school in the nation—his dream come true.

And if he didn't get into MIT? Well, there were plenty

of technical prep schools, but those didn't offer the advanced classes on physics and aerodynamics.

More than anything else, Ethan wanted to fly, maybe be a test pilot . . . or an astronaut! He needed MIT Prep to get there.

His dreams abruptly vanished and Ethan stopped dead in his tracks. The hair on the back of his neck stirred, and he took an involuntary step backward.

Past the next streetlight, two figures stood in the shadows.

As Ethan's eyes adjusted, he recognized them. Who wouldn't? The boy was just as big (although not as tall) as he'd looked in the bleachers, and the skinny girl's hair spiked up like several insect antennae.

The girl was cute, but her face was pointy and her eyes glittered like jagged green glass. The sleeves of her too-big T-shirt were scrunched up to her elbows, showing off well-defined muscles.

The boy cocked his head sideways, examining him. "You Ethan Blackwood?" His voice was soft and a bit higher than Ethan's.

Ethan had at first thought these two might be teen-agers, but seeing them up close and hearing the big guy, he realized they weren't any older than him.

"You're the straight-A student?" the girl asked. "Winner of two science fairs with a dead frog leg and a robot arm?" She made a gag face. "Got a thing for severed limbs?"

Ethan's mouth went dry. In the pit of his stomach something curled inward. Ethan didn't understand. There was nothing to be afraid of in his neighborhood, apart from the occasional spooky bedtime story his mom and dad had told him when he was a kid.

But that scary feeling *was* here.

"I'm Ethan Blackwood." He stood straighter and took a step closer, not wanting to look frightened. "What do you want? An autograph?"

The girl pressed her lips into a white line.

The guy strode to Ethan—making a knuckle-cracking fist.

He swung at Ethan's head!

It took Ethan a split second to react. There were bumps and jostles in a soccer match, all good-natured (more or less). But rougher play landed you in detention and went on your permanent record.

And a *real* fistfight? Anyone stupid enough to throw a punch got shipped off to Sterling Reform School. Or so Ethan had heard. He'd never actually seen it happen.

Ethan had played too many matches, though, *not* to duck.

The boy's fist was half the size of Ethan's head—Ethan got a close look at it (callused knuckles and all) as it whooshed past his nose.

"Hey!" Ethan stumbled back. His hands instinctively rose and balled.

"He's got the reflexes," the girl said. "He even had

them in that antique *mechanical* suit. That will help." She sighed. "And he's the right size, Felix. He's going to have to do."

The boy gave Ethan a doubtful look.

Ethan's fists flattened into a peacemaking gesture. He wanted to turn and run . . . but then something occurred to him. Maybe this was the Westside Warriors' idea of a practical joke. His fear became prickly irritation.

Yes. That had to be it. This was a sore-loser prank. And a bad one.

Well, he wasn't going to give them the satisfaction of seeing him scared.

"What do you mean, I'll 'have to do'?" Ethan demanded.

The large boy's fists dropped to his side (still clenched, though). "Pathetic. There's no fight in him. He's just going to die—or worse, get *us* killed."

"None of them have any fight," the girl said resignedly, "but there's still a chance to save *dozens* of them and the suit. It's worth it."

A block or two away, the thumping bass of music and cheers started. A party.

The big guy looked over his shoulder. "Adults are close, Madison. And this place is watched. We'll have to do this later."

The girl gave Ethan one of those up-and-down glances and shook her head in disgust. She spun around and walked across Mr. Samperson's yard, crushing his primroses.

The big guy followed her.

They vaulted over Mr. Samperson's backyard fence and vanished into the night.

Ethan stood watching, waiting to see if they'd come back, and then he blinked.

Those were two very weird people. He'd have to tell Mom and Dad. He shuddered and shook off his bad feelings. He wasn't going to let some practical joke played by Westside ruin his night. Tonight he was going to enjoy himself. He'd earned it.

Ethan jogged the last two blocks to his house, a blue-and-white Victorian with a wraparound porch . . . where he discovered the source of the music he'd heard.

The party was *here*.

All his teammates, his school friends, and their parents mingled on the porch and on his front lawn. Tiki torches flickered, and a bunch of people waved sparklers. His dad manned the barbecue, and his mom handed out pink lemonades.

There was a banner hung between the live oaks that read:

!!!BLACKWOOD MVP!!! GO, GRIZZZZZLIES!!!

Coach Norman was there too. He raised a lemonade to toast Ethan.

Ethan smiled back. He was sure there was going to be a long lecture about "following the play," even though his kick had won the match. Coach would wait a few days, though. Tonight wasn't the time for lectures.

Ethan's teammates spotted him, and there was another round of lifting him on their shoulders, running around, and growling "Grizzlies!" victory cries.

Ethan really wanted to talk with Mary Vincent (whom he saw with Emma)—but he got caught up for the next half hour talking about the match with Bobby and the rest of the team, figuring out how to win state finals in two weeks.

"Whoa!" Bobby said, glancing at his watch. "I better get some cramming in before bedtime. You know there's going to be a surprise test in pre-algebra tomorrow."

Ethan sighed. Like he could forget that Mr. Lee *always* had a quiz after a match to knock the school's superstar athletes down a notch.

His teammates nodded, realizing it was late for a school night, and their parents started making those little unmistakable hurry-up-let's-go gestures.

They said their goodbyes, and everyone wandered back home.

The party was over.

Ethan noticed Mary Vincent was gone too.

"She left five minutes ago," Emma said from the porch. She flipped her long black hair from her freckled face, then came down and slugged Ethan in the shoulder. "Nice match, by the way. You need a little practice, though, in *other* areas."

"Oh . . . ," Ethan said, frowning.

The one thing he'd hoped for tonight was to talk to Mary, maybe even try to hold her hand (the right way this time).

Or maybe it was too weird? Ethan still couldn't decide if girls were gross . . . or wonderful.

"She's nuts over you, like you didn't know," Emma said, and picked trash off the lawn. "A girl just needs to know she comes first. When you grow up a little more, you'll understand."

Grow up? It wasn't like Ethan was a kid.

Emma was only a year older.

Ethan grabbed the recycle bin and helped her clean up.

Emma had already been accepted into Vassar Prep, one of the best high schools in the world . . . while Ethan would be stuck here. She'd be gone soon, and Ethan wouldn't see her except on holidays.

Ethan liked his brother and sisters (even the twins' constant toddler drooling). He and Emma stuck together no matter what—getting caught stealing chocolate puddings late at night, or accidentally shooting his model rockets into the neighbor's garage. That last stunt had gotten them grounded for a month, and his mom and dad had had to intervene with the School Board of Ethical Behaviors to make sure nothing worse happened.

"Don't worry about Miss Mary Vincent," Emma told him. "You two have a whole year before they even test you for high school. *A lot* can happen in a year."

Before Ethan could protest that a year seemed like a geological era to him, Mom called from inside the house, *"Emmaaaaa!"*

It was bath time, and getting the twins washed, ready for bed, and tucked in took at least two seasoned toddler wranglers.

"I got this." Ethan waved at the litter on the lawn.

"Thanks," Emma said. "Don't let Mary know you're so worried. Us girls can smell the fear!"

Like telling Ethan *not* to be scared of girls was going to make him any less nervous.

Emma bounded up the porch stairs and banged through the front screen door.

She wouldn't be leaving for a month, but Ethan had a weird feeling this would be the last time he'd see her. He wanted to go after her and tell her what a great sister she was and how she was going to show up all those Vassar girls . . . but then he rubbed his shoulder and winced. She hit too hard. He'd have a bruise in the morning.

There'd be plenty of time for that sappy goodbye stuff later.

His throbbing shoulder reminded Ethan of the other slug he'd *almost* taken tonight. To his face!

Those two pale strangers.

What had they called each other? Felix? Madison?

Now that Ethan thought about it, his theory about them being a prank by the Westside Warriors didn't make sense.

What was all that talk about him being "the right size"?
That he'd "have to do"?

That they could "save dozens and the suit"?

He glanced around, half expecting to see them again.

The streets were deserted, though.

Ethan kicked a paper cup into the recycle bin like it was the last shot of the match. He missed.

Had winning tonight been luck or skill? He didn't care—he'd made the shot. The trick next time would be to win without a desperate last-second play.

Superior long-range strategy, Coach was forever telling the team, *always wins over superior immediate tactics.*

Ethan's thoughts about soccer halted as he saw the milk truck turn onto his street. It was early. Deliveries came at four a.m. so the milk was fresh for breakfast.

The white truck doused its headlights and rolled to a stop in front of his house.

Had it broken down? Was something wrong with old Miss Jenkin, the milk lady?

Ethan walked over to see if he could help.

Miss Jenkin didn't get out of the driver's cab—instead, the huge boy, Felix, stepped out and strode toward him.

Ethan didn't understand why he had Miss Jenkin's truck, but he did know there was no way he'd let that guy within fist range again.

Ethan would just yell for his parents. He whirled about—

—and almost ran straight into the pale, spiky-haired girl!

Ethan saw a split-second blur of her hand as she lashed out and hit Ethan dead center in his chest.

He staggered back, sputtering for air. He couldn't even whisper for help.

Felix stood over him, grabbed his arm, and hauled him up.

Ethan finally sucked in a breath to scream for help—but the big guy wrapped a forearm around his throat and squeezed.

"Nuh-uh, small fry," Felix whispered. "Not after making us wait all night."

"What's with the 'small fry' remark?" Madison said, and jabbed Felix in his ribs. "What's that make *me*, then?"

Felix chuckled, and the jiggling motion made Ethan choke. "It makes you a *pip-squeak*," he told her. "A little coral snake, full of venom."

Madison considered this, tapping her lower lip. She then nodded, mollified.

"What are you going to do?" Ethan croaked.

"Shhh . . ." Madison stood on her tiptoes and patted him on the cheek. She motioned Felix to the truck.

He dragged Ethan away.

Ethan tried to keep his legs under him so he wasn't strangled in the process. Panic burned inside him, and he tried to squirm free—yell—anything, but Felix tossed

Ethan into the back of the truck, banging Ethan's head on the side panel so hard that black spots swam in his vision.

Madison ducked inside the truck. "What are we going to do?" she replied. "We're going to see if you have *any* survival instinct left after living in this test tube."

She slammed the door shut behind her and locked it.

The engine rumbled to life, and the truck pulled away from the curb.

Ethan managed to raise his spinning head, blinked through blurred vision, and saw what he thought was his ordinary, happy home . . . one last time.

∘ ∘ ∘ 3 ∘ ∘ ∘

THE INVASION OF EARTH

ETHAN WOKE FROM A DREAMLESS SLEEP.

It was dark. He felt a textured metal floor. He was rocking gently from side to side and smelled bleach and stale milk. His eyes adjusted, and he saw stacks of plastic crates.

He was inside Miss Jenkin's milk truck.

The evening came back to him in a rush: the soccer match—those two strangers—his party—and how the pale boy and girl had grabbed him and tossed him into the truck.

When he'd bumped his head, he must have blacked out. How long?

He probed his scalp, winced, and felt a lump.

Ethan wanted to yell, but he was too scared to make a sound. He scooted into a corner and kept still until he could figure out what was going on.

The truck sped through an intersection, and an overhead streetlamp lit the night. He saw a street sign that read AVENUE K.

Avenue K led to the outskirts of town . . . and farther, into the mountains.

He thought he caught a glimpse of the old lumber mill—but it flashed by too quick.

This truck was definitely breaking the speed limit.

Before the light faded, Ethan spotted the strange girl, Madison, sitting on a crate at the other end of the truck. She was watching him.

"About time," she said, and uncrossed her arms.

She brushed from her eyes the hair that had escaped her spiked ponytail. Her face scrunched as she examined him. She leaned up to the truck's cab and called out, "Looks like he's in one piece . . . more or less."

"Good," a boy said.

Felix. That was the big boy's name. He was driving. He'd grabbed Ethan like he was a rag doll and put him in a choking headlock.

Ethan fought his rising panic as he remembered.

Nothing in school—in his entire life—had prepared him for anything like this. Things like this didn't happen in his neighborhood.

But part of him *did* understand (on what his parents called a "gut level"). He was in real, life-or-death trouble with these two crazy kids.

Wouldn't his parents have noticed him missing after

ten minutes? They'd call his friends, the school, the police, maybe even the mountain search-and-rescue team.

But . . . if no one had seen this milk truck, they'd assume Ethan would be on foot. And if that *had* been the old lumber mill he'd seen back there, he was sixty miles from his house.

How long before anyone looked this far?

He wasn't helpless, though. Ethan could open the back door and jump out. Sure, he might be in the middle of nowhere and have to hide from—

"Don't even think it," Madison said. She eased back on her milk crate and smiled.

Ethan sneaked a hand behind his back and fumbled with the door. It was locked, and his fingers couldn't find the release.

"Even if you got that open and had the nerve to jump," she said, as if she could see right through him, "you'd bounce off the pavement so hard, you'd break every bone in your *stupid* body."

She snorted as if this was funny.

Anger flared inside Ethan. "Is this a joke to you?"

"Not really," she said. "But I am relieved to see you have *some* survival instincts."

That's what she'd said before: "*We're going to see if you have* any *survival instinct left after living in this test tube.*"

See *how?*

And what did she mean, "test tube"?

In a way, this Madison girl was like any other girl in the

seventh grade—cute and annoying all at the same time. But there was a cold, hard thing about her that Ethan had never seen in a girl . . . in anybody.

She looked him over and seemed to decide something.

"I'll tell you what we're doing," she said. "I'll tell you everything. Just promise that you're not going to freak out, okay? I don't want to get rough with you again. It'd defeat the whole purpose of this if I had to break your arms."

Ethan swallowed, recalling how hard she'd hit him—right in the chest with what had felt like a sledgehammer.

Maybe letting her talk was a good thing. In fact, he *ought to* let her and Felix talk all night if he could get them to. That'd give his parents and the police more time to find him.

"You thirsty?" She slid a bottle of chocolate milk across the floor. "Drink that."

Ethan grabbed it, pulled off the aluminum seal, and drank greedily. It was ice-cold and sweet. He felt better.

Madison's nose was a little crooked, like it'd been broken and set not quite right.

No big deal, except Ethan had never seen anyone who'd had a broken bone and hadn't had it perfectly fixed by a school doctor.

Her eyes were the strangest thing, though. They followed his gaze and glittered with a wild intensity.

Madison sat up straight and took a deep breath. "What I'm going to tell you is the truth, but it'll be hard to believe."

From the driver's seat, Felix called back in his soft voice, "Why are you trying? It only works when they *see* it. And then they usually just lose it."

"Shhh!" Madison hissed. "I've got a feeling. This one is different."

She focused back on Ethan. "Where was I . . . ? Oh yeah—fifty years ago the Earth was invaded by aliens. They call themselves the Ch'zar Collective. They came in a ship so big, people said it looked like a second moon in the sky."

What she said confirmed Ethan's assumption: She was *completely nuts.*

"So how come no one ever heard of it?" Ethan asked.

"I'm getting to that." Madison frowned. "It was a 'swarm' ship from another star. It took them hundreds of years to travel here. And when they got near Earth, they broadcast messages of peace in every language."

She had a fact wrong already with her made-up story. There was only one language on Earth. Multiple languages had been outdated and left behind so long ago, it was ancient history.

"When the Ch'zar got into Earth's orbit, they started their invasion. It took them fifty-five seconds to conquer the world."

"Hang on," Ethan said. "Even if they dropped bombs from orbit, it'd take longer than that for them to hit the ground!"

Madison nodded. "Sure, *if* they were using bombs," she

whispered. "But they had a better weapon. Mind control. They took over the brain of every human in the world . . . absorbing it into their Collective."

She waved her hands around her head to indicate this mysterious, totally made-up event.

"People kept all their knowledge and skills," she explained, "but they became slaves to the aliens—controlled and all communicating with some kind of ESP. It was like the billions of humans on Earth ceased to exist and turned into a single . . . *thing*."

She stopped and swallowed and looked sad for a moment.

She must really believe this stuff. Ethan felt sorry for her.

Of course, there had never been a billion people in the world. Today's population was at an all-time high of a couple hundred million. But that was just one more hole in her fairy tale (along with aliens who never existed).

Ethan wondered why Madison and Felix weren't getting help. He'd heard of mental cases that weren't caught with genetic tests and treated early. Those poor people were always placed in hospitals, given medicines to make them feel better . . . and control any violent behavior.

Maybe these two had escaped their hospital.

"One thing went wrong with the Ch'zar's invasion, though," Madison said. "Kids. They were immune to their mind control."

Something bothered Ethan about this part of her story. His forehead wrinkled as he tried to remember his science project on the nervous system.

Then he got it. When puberty hit, there were changes in your brain. Big changes.

One special part of the brain changed a lot. The prefrontal cortex. It did things like help you make good decisions and understand other people.

It was kind of what made you human.

The connection to that scientific fact and Madison's story almost made sense, because kids' brains were different from adults'.

It made Ethan's skin crawl.

"So why are you and I here?" he asked, his tone skeptical. "If aliens control the world, our parents . . . why do I still have to wash the dishes every night?"

Madison slowly shook her head. "At the start, the kids were put into work camps. The aliens kept them there until they grew up, their brains changed, and they got absorbed into the Collective."

Ethan imagined hundreds of thousands of kids losing their parents and going to prisons. How would he feel if he lost his mom and dad like that? It would've been the worst thing in the world.

But he shook off that feeling. This was just a made-up story. An *insane* story.

"The thing was," Madison continued, "when those first kids became part of the Collective, they didn't have the smarts or skills of the other controlled humans. The aliens figured that humans had to be raised in a *natural* environment to be as smart and creative as possible."

She reached behind her and pulled out a manila folder.

It was a school record. Ethan had seen them a million times before. It held teachers' notes, your extracurricular activities, medical records, and every test score. It's what high schools looked at when they decided to accept you (or not).

Basically, it contained your entire life—past, present, and future.

"That's when they built the neighborhoods," Madison said. "Places where 'parents' could raise their kids in an ideal environment until they were old enough to be taken." She licked her lips. "This is the hard part, and I'm really, really sorry . . . but you live in a pretty, suburban test tube."

Ethan stopped listening, because he saw BLACKWOOD, ETHAN printed on the folder in her hands.

"Hey, that's mine!" he cried, and lunged for her.

4

A GOOD REASON TO FREAK OUT

MADISON THREW OUT AN ARM AND KNOCKED Ethan back.

"Got to be quicker than that, Blackwood," she said.

"You're not supposed to have that!"

Madison shrugged. "What can I say? Your school has lousy security. Two locked doors and a jimmied file cabinet and we had access to *everyone's* records."

No one was supposed to read that stuff. It was personal and superconfidential.

She flipped through the pages. " 'Ethan Gregor Blackwood,' " she read. " 'Age twelve. Ranked in the top third percentile in standardized tests. Strong aptitude for science.' Oh—here's something I missed—'homemade pyrotechnics shot into a neighbor's garage'? 'Disciplinary action required'?"

She leaned back to talk to Felix. "See? I was right. We've got a chance with this one."

Madison's gleeful expression cooled as she returned to the file. "Only two sisters and one brother? That's . . . different."

Ethan looked away and flushed.

All the other kids in his neighborhood had eight or nine siblings by the time their parents were middle-aged. When Ethan was growing up, they'd all teased him and Emma—calling them "shorties" or "dodos"—like they were genetic dead ends.

That's why he'd tried so hard to be popular and good at soccer and to get the highest scores on every test . . . to show them how wrong they were.

He'd been relieved when the twins had come along the year before last.

"It's funny," Madison said. "I wonder what makes *your* parents so different."

Ethan was about to tell her to mind her own business— that his dad and mom were perfectly normal—but the truck stopped.

Felix hopped out and opened the rear door.

Ethan inhaled fresh cold air and smelled pine.

The milk truck was at the end of a dirt road carved into a steep mountain slope. In the distance were the twinkling lights of Santa Blanca.

Ethan had been to these foothills on family picnics.

The mountains, though, were off-limits. There were supposed to be real grizzly bears and cougars here. Some kids got lost up here once and were eaten (or so the stories went).

He backed into the truck and revised his guess about how far he was from home. It had to be a hundred miles.

No one would find him out here.

Felix scanned the night sky and the glowing band of the Milky Way. "We better hurry," he said. "We're lucky to have gotten this far, but the moon will be out in a half hour. They'll have enough light to spot us."

They? Felix must mean his alien bogeymen.

Madison pushed past Ethan and jumped out of the truck. She tossed him a white coat. "Take it," she said, "or you'll freeze."

Felix offered a large hand to help Ethan. "We're on foot from here, friend."

Ethan imagined fighting his way past these two—but what was to stop Felix from grabbing him, as before, and dragging him along in a killer stranglehold?

He'd play along and wait for his chance to make a break for it.

"I'm not your friend," Ethan told him. He climbed out of the truck without taking Felix's offered hand.

Goose bumps dotted his arms. It *was* cold up here. Ethan reluctantly shrugged into the white parka Madison had tossed him. It had a patch with Blanca Dairy's logo: a ridiculous smiling cow holding out a big glass of milk.

Madison forged a trail through the woods, going up the mountain.

Felix nodded at Ethan and pointed after her.

Of course they were going to put him *between* them. It'd be easier to keep an eye on him. Harder for him to escape.

He started, turned to Felix, and said, "Your story's *crazy.*"

"Yeah. But true," Felix said, moving alongside him and crushing the underbrush like a bull. "You'll see."

Ethan's heart raced, and he wanted to make a break into the woods. Just run. As far and as fast as he could. If Felix didn't pounce on him, Ethan was sure he could outrun him. Superfast Madison, though, might catch him.

Ethan took a deep breath to steady himself. He'd wait. He knew there'd be a better chance to escape . . . but he'd probably only get *one* chance.

They trudged up the forested slope. There was a game trail, but it was dark, and Ethan stumbled and tripped.

Felix and Madison seemed to be able to see in the dark.

"I don't get why aliens would need us," Ethan said, trying to start up the conversation again. "I mean, if they had the science to travel between stars, what do they want with mind-controlled human slaves? That's like using horses to plow fields instead of tractors."

"They use *everything,*" Felix told him. "We think they're building another starship, maybe more than one. It's like when a beehive gets too big, it splits into two . . . or an amoeba that absorbs everything in its path, then divides in half. What's that called? Fission, right?"

Felix was smarter than he looked. He was as crazy as Madison, but definitely not dumb.

Ethan wouldn't underestimate his strength or brains.

Felix continued, "The Ch'zar use armies of humans and robots as laborers and researchers, and to add to their total brainpower. When you think about it, it's pretty much as efficient as you can get."

That did kind of make sense.

For a second, Ethan imagined the aliens going from star to star, taking over every world, multiplying, and spreading throughout the galaxy. He shuddered.

"Okay," Ethan said, "if that's true, then how can you two be here? Why aren't you in a 'neighborhood' being raised until you're old enough to get mind-controlled?"

"Not all the adults were taken when the Ch'zar invaded," Felix said. "Some were far underground and were shielded from their mind powers." Felix stood straighter and proudly declared, "My grandparents and parents were Resistance fighters. Madison and I are third-generation Resisters."

Ethan admired the weird way they'd built their story. It was a self-supporting collection of lies. There was no way you could poke a hole in it. Totally insane . . . but airtight.

Madison halted. "Ridge is ahead," she whispered.

The forest broke twenty paces in front of them. There

was more rocky slope, and then nothing but the horizon and stars beyond.

Madison and Felix stood still and listened, and then Felix whispered back, "I think it'll be safe. We'll show him and then make for the cave and the suits."

"Roger that," she replied.

Something had just changed between Madison and Felix. There was a crisp formality that hadn't been there a second ago.

Ethan had a sinking feeling the time for talk was over. Whatever they had planned for him was about to happen.

He looked around: nothing but endless dark trees in a sea of shadows (and him in that stupid, easy-to-spot white parka).

Felix set a massive hand on Ethan's shoulder. "We go up," he said, and gently but firmly shoved Ethan ahead . . . and he didn't take his hand off.

They marched out of the woods, up the slope, and to the top of the ridge.

The full moon crested the horizon. Silver light touched the mountaintops and flooded the plains below.

Icy wind whipped Ethan's face, and he had to blink away tears.

Ethan had known there were roads and farmland and wind turbines out there. It was a clear night, so he should have been able to see Haven Heart, the next city, fifty miles away.

But the world didn't look like the world he knew. There were no forests, grasslands, or fields of wheat.

The land was barren. Dust devils whipped around, and it looked like pictures he'd seen of Mars.

Giants walked this unfamiliar landscape.

Machines half a mile long with segmented bodies chewed through the foothills and carved deep channels, grinding and extracting acres of rock and soil with massive mechanical teeth. Dirt poured into these factories that looked like centipedes, where smelters glowed white-hot and spewed smoke and molten metal.

Ethan was stunned senseless and felt as if he was drowning (probably because he was so shocked, he forgot to breathe).

Clustered about these walking factories were hundreds of smaller robots, making repairs and carrying off red-hot ingots with eight spiderlike forklift pincers. They deposited their cargo into six-wheeled trucks that looked like toys at this distance, but Ethan figured they were the size of a city block.

Those trucks moved in a constant stream to the horizon, where their headlights curved up into the sky . . . as if the road went all the way into orbit.

Ethan's gaze drifted to what he had first assumed was a cloud, but he now saw it had a smooth, silver, curved surface dotted with hexagonal holes. It had ripples and ridges . . . like it'd been grown in a cocoon, or like it was a hive.

From this floating structure, tiny figures emerged. They dropped into the air and plummeted toward the earth.

Ethan took a step back . . . and stumbled.

Felix braced him.

The objects arced up before they hit the ground—following the contours of the earth—up the mountain slope—straight toward them.

"Drones . . . ," Madison whispered.

"They've spotted us," Felix said. "Get to the cave. Fast!"

Madison grabbed Ethan's hand. "Come on, dummy!" she shouted. "Run!"

5

THREE OF THEM

ETHAN COULDN'T MOVE.

Fear solidified into a concrete chunk inside him. He could only stare, eyes wide with terror at the drones that rocketed up the mountainside toward him . . . growing larger every second.

They were like the model rockets he and Emma had built. Sleek and gray, fins on the tails, blooms of near-invisible heat from the back, and something else, a shimmering on their sides.

Six drones veered left—faster than any rocket Ethan had ever seen—and circled him.

He spun and caught a glimpse of membranes along their sides. Wings?

He also spotted slender insect legs drawn in close to their bodies.

"You idiot!" Madison screamed. "Move!"

She threw herself at Ethan and tackled him. They landed in the dirt—her on top of him.

A line of darts thunked into the ground next to Ethan's head.

Each dart was two feet long and black, and on the exposed end a sack pumped venom like a bee's stinger . . . only a hundred times bigger.

"Get up!" Madison whispered. "Or they'll catch you."

She jumped to her feet and ran.

Ethan, still dazed, watched Madison sprint off—then focused on the living darts that had nearly impaled him and on the drones overhead.

Felix stood ten paces away. He shouted and jumped, trying to get their attention.

He got it.

They spiraled over his head.

Felix tossed what looked like a baseball into the air.

It exploded with a brilliant flash and a bang.

The drones scattered, stunned and blind—one flew straight into the ground with a crunch and lay there twitching and gushing green goo.

Felix gestured for Ethan to follow, and then he turned and ran too.

Ethan didn't know what those flying things were . . . but he *did* know he wanted to live.

Ethan got up and ran.

He raced past Felix, caught halfway up to Madison, and then hesitated when she ran *into* an outcropping of rock and vanished.

A shadow wavered where she'd disappeared.

Ethan ran up to the rock and found a camouflaging tarp. He brushed it aside and saw a narrow cave entrance.

He ducked inside.

Felix lumbered in after him, pushed Ethan back, and spun around to look out.

Satisfied with what he saw, Felix drew the curtain closed.

It went pitch-dark.

Ethan heard Felix panting. Madison too. He felt his blood thundering through his body, got dizzy, and sank to his knees.

"Secure the back," Felix whispered to Madison. "Set the perimeter charges."

"You got it," Madison replied. She scrambled into the darkness.

"Take a second, Ethan," Felix said in his soft voice. "Catch your breath. We'll have a few minutes to talk while the drones expand their search pattern. But then we'll make a break for it. Do you understand?"

"No," Ethan said. "I don't understand anything."

A tube glowing ghostly yellow flickered to life in Felix's hand.

This light showed a jagged tunnel that went deeper into the mountain.

"Come," Felix said, and moved farther in. "Ask your questions . . . and I'll have a few of my own to ask you, too."

Ethan looked at the curtain. Beyond, the buzzing of more drones grew fainter. There was no way he'd go back out there . . . so he followed Felix.

Ten paces winding through solid rock, and they emerged in a chamber so large that Felix's light vanished in darkness.

Felix sat on a boulder next to three huge shapes covered by more of those camouflaging tarps.

Ethan's legs turned rubbery. He sat suddenly in the dirt.

"I—I don't get it," Ethan said. "I've been to Haven Heart, Port Amber, and Junesville. I've gone on field trips to the National Museum of Art and the Grand Oceanarium. There've been out-of-town soccer matches. Next week I'm supposed to go to the state finals. . . ."

He rubbed his face. He knew this was no dream, but he wasn't sure it was all real, either.

Or maybe *he* was the one going crazy?

"If what you've told me is true," Ethan said, "how come I never saw any of those factories or those bugs out there?"

"You were on buses for these field trips?" Felix said.

"Sure. School buses."

"And after you went through the Geo-Transit Tunnel out of Santa Blanca?"

"I saw farms and wind turbines. There were cattle herds. Fruit stands."

"All the windows on the bus were up? The air-conditioning on?"

"Yes, but what's that got to do with anything?"

"The windows on your buses are transparent computer screens," Felix explained. "They show you what they want you to see. The air conditioner is full of gas that puts you to sleep."

Ethan remembered those bus rides. Superboring. And he always slept . . . waking only when they got to another city.

"But I've seen pictures of Paris and Rome and the Great Wall of China," Ethan protested. "Those places aren't neighborhoods like you're talking about."

"The pictures in your books and newspapers were taken fifty years ago," Felix said.

"No way," Ethan said.

"Haven't you ever wondered," Felix asked and leaned closer, "why the computers in your classes are linked through your school's network, but not connected to other cities like Paris or Hong Kong?"

"Because it'd be expensive?" Ethan tried.

Felix shook his head. "Because *they* control the news, the textbooks, everything you see or hear . . . or know."

Madison stepped from the shadows. The darkness seemed to cling to her.

"Is he ready?" she asked. "Did you show him?"

"No," Felix told her, irritated with her impatience.

Ethan could only stare at Madison, his mouth open.

She wasn't in her jeans and T-shirt. A skintight body-suit hugged her form, covering everything but her arms and calves. Her suit was emerald green and had veins like a leaf.

She sat next to Felix and dug into a duffel bag. She got out a pair of black boots and pulled them on. She then found a pair of elbow-length black gloves and snugged them on too.

"Charges are set," she told Felix. "We lost the drones . . . but that's never a sure thing for long."

"Understood," Felix said.

Felix pulled off his shirt. Underneath, he wore a simi-lar, navy blue bodysuit. Like Madison, he pulled on gloves and boots.

"Let's cut to the chase, Blackwood." Madison faced Ethan and put her hands on her hips. "We need your help. We can sneak out of this mess—but it's going to take all three of us to move the suits."

She stood and pulled a camouflaging cloth off the three large objects behind them.

They weren't rocks.

Underneath were insects—three *big* insects!

Ethan got up and stumbled back. Watery terror flooded through his arms and legs. He fell on his butt.

One of the bugs had to be the largest rhinoceros beetle that ever existed. It stood upright, fifteen feet tall on its oversized, spike-encrusted hind legs. Its head curved up to form two barbed horns.

The monster bug's exoskeleton shifted color from navy

blue to midnight black, depending on what angle Ethan stared at it from. It had a dozen tiny eyes . . . that stared back at him.

It *was* a real bug . . . but not entirely, because on its abdomen was a seam—segments of armor plate, and tiny letters that read:

WARNING: !!!EXTREME HYDRAULIC PRESSURE!!!
OPEN WITH MINIMUM IMPACT TORQUE 40,000 PSI.

The second bug was a gold ant smaller than the beetle, about the size of a car. It crouched and looked ready to pounce.

Black stripes covered its gold armor. It didn't have giant jaws like a regular ant. Instead, the head tapered back into a sweeping helmet that covered most of its thorax (that was the word Ethan remembered from biology class for an insect's chest). Also, an ant's thorax and abdomen normally joined at a narrow point, but on this one the two fused smoothly together.

While the black-and-gold ant definitely looked alive, with sensor hairs that bristled and flicked along every part of its body, it also had machine parts. Tiny amber lights winked along the underside of its abdomen, and there were recessed forward-facing scoops that reminded Ethan of air intakes he'd seen in pictures of old fighter jets.

The hind and middle legs were small compared to the massive front limbs. Those had three large segments, each with wicked rakes and barbs that looked like they'd been designed to tear flesh off bones.

But the thing that made Ethan involuntarily scoot back in fear was the stinger that extended from its rear. It was six feet long . . . smoldering with heat.

And pointed at Ethan.

He felt it looking at him, *into* him. It was thinking, too. Ethan swore it felt like the bug was trying to figure out what *he* was, just like he was trying to figure out what *it* was . . . and it was deciding if it should attack him. Ethan wasn't sure how he knew what an insect was thinking— but he knew!

The last nightmare creature was a dragonfly twice as long as the ant.

It was sleek and smooth and black. There were camou-flaging patches of emerald green on its exoskeleton that shifted as Ethan watched.

Its wings shimmered with rainbow patterns. The thing's eyes were huge—two soccer-ball-sized orbs that enveloped its head . . . and Ethan found himself unable to *not* stare into them.

Ethan wanted to scream—or run—or hide . . . but all he managed was to stammer, "Wh-wh-what are they?"

Felix approached the beetle. "The Ch'zar mutated insects when they first arrived here," he said. "They use exoskeleton fighting suits like these in combat."

The beetle waggled its antennae at Felix.

"They enhance your strength and speed," Felix said,

"and have sensors and weapons systems." He stepped between the ant and the dragonfly. "Each has a different specialization. Together they're an unstoppable team."

Ethan shook his head, not *quite* terrified anymore . . . but not understanding a word Felix said.

"We've learned to tame them," Madison told Ethan, "adapted their fit, and turned them against the Ch'zar."

"You . . . use them?" Ethan looked at the bugs, then at Felix and Madison, and an uneasy feeling twisted in his stomach. "So if there are three of them, shouldn't there be three of you?"

"We *were* three," Madison whispered, and she looked away.

"We lost one of our team," Felix said. He tried to say more . . . then glanced at Madison and couldn't seem to get the words out.

Ethan didn't know what to say. "I'm very sorry," he said. "He died?"

"None of that matters, Blackwood," Madison snapped. "Our mission priority is getting out of here in one piece."

She pointed at the titanic ant. "You're taking that one. It's a good unit. It can be a little temperamental, but it should be easy for *you*, since you're used to wearing one of those idiotic athletic suits."

Ethan got to his feet and brushed the dirt off his back. He was feeling less terrified and more annoyed at these two—or maybe annoyed at himself, because he *still* wasn't getting what they were asking him to do.

"How am I supposed to take that . . . that *thing*?" He tried to conceal his revulsion (and failed).

Felix went to the beetle and set his hands on its belly.

To Ethan's utter amazement, the seam on the exoskeleton hinged, automatically pulling apart, and sections slid aside to reveal its insides.

Only it wasn't guts and ichor like he expected in a living creature.

Inside was a contoured surface that matched Felix's back. There were a dozen hexagonal monitors and a thousand blinking lights and colored indicators. Every surface pulsed as if it was breathing.

Felix stepped into the first joints of the insect's oversized middle legs and slipped his hands into the upper pair of limbs.

The beetle's exoskeleton closed around Felix with a series of clicks.

He stood before Ethan looking like part medieval knight in black-blue armor and part gigantic insect.

It was fascinating *and* completely gross at the same time.

"There is no way . . . ," Ethan said, turning to Madison.

Madison wasn't paying attention to him. Her head cocked to one side, listening.

There were distant bumps—then a tremor.

"The perimeter charges!" Madison shouted.

Felix's amplified voice boomed from the beetle. "We didn't lose the drones. Mount up, Blackwood. Get into your suit!"

"What—!"

"You can be drafted into this fight," Felix told him, "or you can be a *casualty*."

Madison ran to the dragonfly. She set both hands on its sleek body, and it opened like the beetle's. Only instead of standing, she had to lie flat inside.

It quickly sealed around her.

The dragonfly took to the air, hovering with a barely audible whisper from blurred wings.

The tarp over the cave entrance ripped away. Moonlight flooded in.

Thirty-foot-long metal prongs pierced the tunnel, sparking and wrenching and sending cracks through the surrounding rock.

Ethan got a glimpse of a mechanical face outside—a dozen cameras and spotlights that peered into the crevice and focused on him.

It was one of those spider robots that tended the moving factories.

Only here, up close, Ethan saw this robot was the size of a three-story house.

And it tore through the mountainside to get to him!

The rhinoceros beetle crouched. Guns and missile pods popped out from recesses in its exoskeleton. Laser-targeting sights tracked through the dusty air and settled on the mechanical intruder.

"Move it!" Felix roared at Ethan.

Ethan hesitated for a heartbeat, then ran to the gigantic ant.

It went against every instinct to crawl inside this thing . . . instincts that screamed at Ethan to run away.

Those same instincts, though, when he saw tons of rock crumbling around him, and the robot about to smash him flat, decided that the ant was the better of the two options.

"Okay," he told himself. "Get your head in the game, Blackwood."

Ethan touched the surface of the armor.

It was smooth and golden and had a static-charged, sticky feel to it.

But unlike when Felix and Madison had touched their suits, the ant's exoskeleton (maybe the only thing that could save Ethan's life now) sat unmoving.

∘ ∘ ∘ 6 ∘ ∘ ∘

FIGHTING SUIT

ETHAN POUNDED ON THE ANT. ALL THAT DID was bruise his hand.

A chunk of rock big enough to squash a truck fell next to Ethan and showered him with stinging gravel.

He hammered furiously on the armor—then did so with *both* hands.

That did something, because the creature twitched, and its antennae flicked at him.

Its eyes tracked him with a golden stare as if it had just now made up its mind to accept Ethan's puny presence.

The ant's limbs moved slightly. Ethan stepped back from their flesh-ripping barbs.

There was a click. Armor sections in the abdomen popped open and rotated away. Other pieces of the ant's armor parted with a hiss and pulled back.

Inside was a contoured couch with minimal padding. There were a dozen hexagonal computer view screens set at odd angles. There were blinking lights with foreign letters jumbled about them. Tiny holes set in the sides seemed to exhale.

Behind him, the spider robot tore through the wall, wrenching away a chunk of rock that must have weighed fifty tons and tossing it aside like it was a beach ball.

In the blink of an eye, Madison's dragonfly darted past the machine and out into the open air.

There was no time to waste. Any shred of doubt Ethan had about climbing into the insect vanished. If he stayed out here, he'd get crushed.

Ethan backed into the cockpit, setting one leg and then the other into the hollow insect limbs, and then reached for its arms.

Even before he got his hands in place, the suit closed around him.

A second contoured piece rotated around his front and pressed in place. A liquid filled the insect's limbs. It was squishy . . . and then Ethan couldn't feel his hands or feet anymore. Pinpricks crawled up his arms and legs and gave them that "falling asleep" sensation up to his spine.

He panicked and squirmed, feeling like he was smothering—and then the view screens came on and fresh air blasted in from the vents.

Three screens in front showed a panoramic view—a

smaller screen showed the ant's back—one fixed on the stinger—one locked onto Felix's beetle—and three tracked the giant spider machine.

What would happen if he had to look up or down?

When Ethan thought this, the cameras shifted as if he had turned his own head.

It had to have guessed what he wanted—or if the Ch'zar had mind-control technology, could this part-living, part-machine ant have *read* his thoughts?

Felix's voice came from a speaker. "I'll take care of this guy. Move out after me."

The spider robot reached for them with huge, crushing hydraulic pincers.

Felix's beetle jumped at the machine.

He closed the distance in a single bound—hit the robot's metal frame—and punched *through* the body of the machine.

One of Ethan's view screens automatically zoomed and showed the beetle ripping chunks of solid steel from the robot's spider body like it was Styrofoam.

But two more robots appeared behind that first one and pushed past it, tearing into the mountainside—coming straight for Ethan!

How do I make this thing move?

Ethan's heart raced, sweat trickled down his sides, and he hyperventilated.

It was like the first time he'd been strapped into an athletic suit—he'd freaked out then, too. But Coach hadn't taken him out. He'd told Ethan he had to work through it or he'd never get inside one of the suits again.

That's what he had to do now. Work through his fear.

If this Ch'zar fighting suit was anything like the athletic suit he'd played soccer in, then all Ethan had to do was move his legs and arms like he was running or jumping, and the machine would translate his motion into action.

He tried it.

The instant he took a step forward, the suit seemed to anticipate—*jumping* through the opening and landing fifty feet away on open ground.

It happened so fast. Ethan twisted his head around, trying to get his bearings.

Spider robots and Felix's beetle and the flash of dragonfly wings whipped across his view screens.

On one screen, though, a pincer leg got bigger and bigger, aimed right at him!

Ethan threw up his arms—and caught it.

It had hit him, but instead of it skewering the ant, Ethan had stopped it.

He struggled with the enormous weight . . . and held it immobilized.

"Ha!" Ethan grunted in triumph.

He pulled the spider robot closer and (even though he thought it'd be impossible) tossed it aside like it was a toy.

All hundred tons of metal went flying end over end,

landed on its back—skidded across the ridge—and into an-other robot. It knocked down that spider robot like a bowling pin, and both of them went over the edge of the mountain.

For a split second, Ethan felt like he'd just kicked a match-winning goal.

Then he remembered where he was. This wasn't a game.

More robots crawled onto the top of the mountain.

Ethan's view screens focused on that floating hive ship as it drifted closer . . . and more drones dropped free and rocketed toward them.

Felix's beetle landed next to him. "Stay close," he told Ethan over the radio.

Ethan was panting, too much in shock to reply.

The beetle ducked its head and pointed its horns at the closest robot. Lightning flashed between the beetle's horns, and lasers appeared, intersected, and shot out in a single sparkling beam that hit the machine.

It blasted a smoldering hole in the spider robot's body big enough to drive a bus through.

The mechanical monstrosity tumbled off the ridge.

"We have *lasers*?" Ethan cried.

"You and Madison have lasers," Felix said. "That was a class-C particle beam. Targets at three o'clock—blast 'em!"

Ethan turned. A robot scrambled toward him.

He had no idea how to use his suit's lasers . . . but he narrowed his eyes and focused his fear at the incoming machine.

Targeting circles appeared on-screen, spun, and locked on the approaching figure.

The suit's stinger curled toward the enemy.

There was a blast of heat that Ethan felt inside the suit.

A ruby red beam cut through the air, illuminating the thin nighttime mist, and sliced off five of the spider robot's legs.

The machine tumbled and ground to a halt.

Madison's voice came over the speakers: "That was just the welcoming committee. They're deploying warrior 'bots."

Her dragonfly flew through a swarm of drones—so fast Ethan barely tracked her.

She dodged and spun. Lasers flashed from her forward-pointing pincers, leaving smoldering drone wreckage that fell from the air.

The dragonfly rocketed toward the floating hive.

A red warning light buzzed over another screen, and Ethan saw a new type of spider robot climb over the ridge. This one was black and red and twice as big as the others. It had sixteen hydraulically powered pincer legs. It ran toward him, quickly building speed.

Felix was nowhere in sight.

Ethan would have to defend himself.

He spun around, crouched, and jumped.

His fighting suit landed on the mechanical monster's body. He grabbed its head with serrated limbs and—before the robot could swat him—jumped away, ripping off the metal head.

He dropped the mass of steel.

And then realized his mistake.

He had jumped away, all right . . . probably avoided getting squished. But when he'd jumped off the robot, he'd jumped *too* far—over the edge of the ridge. He was falling toward the valley floor a thousand feet below.

He clutched at the air, instinctually grasping, trying to swim, or flap wings that weren't there—useless!

The world spun on his view screens . . . except those cameras focused on his back. There, the armor split and wings flicked out—diamond membranes that became a blur.

He snapped to a stop and hovered.

"I can fly?" Ethan whispered, amazed.

Then he understood. This suit of armor wasn't an ant.

It was a *wasp*.

He imagined himself moving the muscles on his back and running, jumping—anything to make him go up.

He flew higher over the ridge.

This was so cool. Hadn't he always wanted to fly?

He spotted Madison's dragonfly, and his happiness faded.

She was in trouble.

Emerging from the floating hive were wasps. Not like Ethan's. These were black and red and half his size . . . but there were *ten* of them.

Her dragonfly veered from the hive and the wasps. She barrel rolled, dodging the lasers flashing from their stingers.

One laser hit her and stitched a smoldering line down the side of her dragonfly.

"Incoming!" she cried over the speakers.

Ethan spotted Felix's beetle. He was in trouble, too.

He was on the ridge. Clawing into the clearing around him were three smaller rhinoceros beetles. Instead of attacking, Felix slowly retreated.

"Fall back," Felix ordered. "Both of you—before *more* reinforcements come."

A hundred thoughts whirled through Ethan's mind, none coming to rest.

He rose higher into the air.

Those other insects weren't after him . . . probably because they hadn't seen him yet.

But could there be another reason? Ethan had just been in the wrong place at the wrong time. He'd been dragged into this fight.

Was it even *his* fight?

He glanced at the forested side of the mountains, down to the valley, and at Santa Blanca. Its streetlights twinkled peacefully, everyone in his neighborhood unaware of the battle up here.

Like it wasn't a part of this violent, alien world.

"Ethan!" Felix said over the radio. "Fall back. We can escape if you help!"

Felix blasted one smaller beetle with his particle beam. It exploded backward and hit the mountainside, leaving a smoldering crater . . . from which it got up and crept forward.

Escape.

Hadn't just ten minutes ago Ethan been looking for a chance to escape Felix and Madison?

He hadn't asked them to show him any of this.

He hadn't asked to fight the Ch'zar.

All he wanted was to go back to his normal old life—truth or no truth.

He wanted to wake up and find out this was a dream.

Madison. Felix. Those two had hit and kidnapped him.

Maybe they weren't the good guys. And maybe the bugs weren't the bad guys. Maybe everything they'd told him was a lie.

Ethan trusted only three people in the world: his dad, his mom, and his sister.

He had to tell his parents and Emma about this. They'd help him figure it out.

Madison cried, "Blackwood? Are you there? Are you okay?"

"No," Ethan whispered.

He turned and flew toward Santa Blanca.

Go home, he thought to the suit. *Fly as fast as you can!*

Something clicked on either side of the suit.

On-screen Ethan saw jet engines pop out from the wasp's abdomen. They exploded with fury and fire and shot the wasp through the air like a rocket.

○ ○ ○ 7 ○ ○ ○

YOU FORGOT SOMETHING

BLINDING SUNLIGHT STREAMED THROUGH Ethan's bedroom window. His alarm clock buzzed like an angry wasp.

He rolled over and slapped the snooze button.

It was fifteen minutes *after* his alarm usually went off. Had it been buzzing all this time?

He sat up and swung his legs out of bed.

Every muscle in his body ached. He felt like he'd played three soccer matches, worked out in the gym, and run forty laps around the practice field.

He unbuttoned his pajama top (which was covered with rocket ships and astronauts) and found bruises on his chest and arms.

He ran his fingers over the yellowing black circles and scrapes.

If your athletic suit didn't have a perfect fit, you got

rattled around during a match. Ethan had seen new kids on the team come out of a soccer game looking like they'd been beaten up.

But nothing like *this*.

Besides, Ethan's suit had been fine-tuned to fit just before last night's match.

Emma had punched him in the shoulder, but that couldn't have—

Ethan saw the flash of a big fist aimed right at his nose—then it turned into a huge fist of steel, as big as his room . . . and he'd caught that one with his own hands.

He blinked. Where had *that* memory come from?

It had to have been part of a dream. Now that he thought about it, though, he couldn't remember what he'd dreamed last night.

He stood and stretched. Aches and pains creaked up and down his legs. When he looked, he saw more bruises there than on his arms.

He glanced around for some clue to what might've happened to him.

Everything looked just the way it should. White shirts and ties and pressed slacks hung in his closet. Folded jeans and T-shirts sat on his dresser for after school. His schoolbooks and the high school catalogs he'd been browsing sat on shelves. Even Mr. Bubbles, his pet betta fish, looked normal as he darted to the top of his tank for his breakfast pellet.

Ethan paused. Something disturbed him as he watched the fish's organic blue curves.

Weird.

He went to his desk and picked up the framed picture of his mom and dad, him, and Emma. They cradled the just-born twins. It had been taken two years ago. It was hard to believe Dana and Danny had grown up so fast. But that was a good thing. Their potty training was starting to take. Dirty-diaper duty was one thing Ethan would be happy to see go.

He would figure out what had happened later. He got dressed for school.

Ethan noticed the clothes he'd worn last night had been tossed in the corner.

Funny . . . he was never that sloppy.

From his open bedroom door, Emma cleared her throat.

"What happened last night?" she asked. "I covered for you. Told Mom and Dad you'd gone to sleep. Do you know how much trouble we'd *both* be in if they figured out it was just two pillows in your bed?"

Ethan studied his sister. She wasn't making any sense.

She was dressed in her school skirt and white blouse. Her black hair was pulled back into a ponytail, her arms crossed over her chest, and her normally sparkling eyes narrowed with worry. She was serious.

"How late was I out?" Ethan asked, not entirely sure he wanted to hear the answer.

"Don't be a jerk. You know you got in after midnight. If Mom and Dad found out—or the School Board—you'd get detention until you graduated. *If* they let you graduate!"

Ethan gulped. His sister was a practical joker, but she wouldn't kid around about something like this.

"I don't remember," he whispered. "Really. I don't."

Emma sighed. "Okay. Fine. Don't tell me. But if you were with Mary Vincent, you're going to get her in trouble, too."

"But I wasn't . . ."

Ethan was about to say he wasn't with Mary, but he did remember *a* girl. Not Mary. The girl he imagined had an angular face, kind of cute, spiky hair . . . a mean stare.

Ethan spotted the suitcase that Emma had dragged down the hall.

"What's that for?" he asked.

"Oh . . . I don't remember," she said with maximum sarcasm. Then she smiled and relented. "Well, word has it that a certain Miss Blackwood got Early Honors Admission at Vassar. One of the other six honor students got sick, and since I was the first alternate on the list . . ." She beamed. "So instead of going next month like I was supposed to, I'm leaving tomorrow on the Geo-Transit train! I'll get four weeks to meet teachers, get a head start on studying, and have first pick of the dorm rooms. It'll look supercool on my record."

"That's great!" Ethan said. He went to hug his sister.

She hesitated a moment—deciding if she was still mad at him or not—then decided not, and hugged him back.

"You've got to help me figure out what to take," she said. "There's not a lot of time." She glanced into his room and added, "Speaking of which . . . why aren't you ready for school? Don't you have a test today? Or did Mr. Lee stop torturing his jock students?"

"Mr. Lee!" Ethan smacked his head. "I forgot all about his pre-algebra quiz!"

He raced back to his desk.

Thankfully, his notes and flash cards were all there.

"Hurry up." Emma started down the hallway. "Mom made pancakes and bacon. There won't be any leftovers for slowpokes."

Ethan flipped through his flash cards, reviewing how to graph a parabola, how to convert fractions into decimals. He barely knew this stuff. Why hadn't he crammed last night?

He couldn't concentrate.

He'd think better with food in his stomach. Maybe Mom would let him review while eating. She didn't approve of him studying at the dining table, but this time she might make an exception. She knew he couldn't afford to mess up anything before state finals.

He headed downstairs . . . but paused to get those wadded-up clothes. Ethan couldn't stand seeing such a mess.

He grabbed the crumpled jeans and his red Grizzlies

T-shirt—then stopped, feeling like someone had dumped a cup of ice water down his back.

Under the clothes was a parka.

It was the kind you'd put on to go out in a blizzard for a snowball fight. Or maybe something you'd wear into a walk-in freezer. It was white except for the sleeves, which were covered in gray-green slime to the elbows.

Ethan turned it over. There was a patch on the chest. It had an embroidered cow holding a big glass of milk. The cow had a ridiculously large milk mustache.

It was the logo of Blanca Dairy, where they got their . . .

. . . milk.

Delivered by Miss Jenkin in her white milk truck.

Ethan suddenly remembered everything that had *really* happened last night.

○ ○ ○ 8 ○ ○ ○

ETHAN'S PARENTS

ETHAN TOUCHED THE GOO ON THE PARKA'S sleeve. It was oily and smelled of fried food and honey.

This was the stuff that had oozed from inside the wasp armor's limbs.

He shuddered and pulled his hand away.

Ethan remembered—

—starting from when he'd left the battle on the mountaintop.

He'd flown away fast! It had taken only minutes to soar back down the mountain—over the valley—to the out-skirts of Santa Blanca—over his street—and his house—which, before he blinked, he'd overshot by three blocks.

He'd touched down instead in the biggest open spot he saw—the soccer field.

The wasp had hit and tumbled and crashed into the goal.

His impact had crumpled the painted green titanium soccer field like it was tinfoil, and wrecked the goal.

It had been so late at night, no one was around, but Ethan knew *someone* would've heard that crash landing and come looking.

He felt like he had been beaten up. He somehow, though, found the strength to limp the wasp to the gardener's shed behind the gym.

He had the wasp snap off the padlock, then entered and maneuvered into the corner of the shed—pushing aside the tractor mower like it was an empty cardboard box.

When he tried to get out of the suit, he realized Felix had never told him how.

He panicked and struggled and then stopped, exhausted.

That was when he spotted a blinking red light with a weird symbol. Ethan couldn't read it, but the symbol looked like the armor segment that had moved to access the cockpit.

He tapped it a few times.

The light changed from red to amber to green. The abdomen cracked and automatically opened.

He scrambled out. Quick.

The wasp armor shut behind him.

Ethan gulped in fresh air, even though the gardener's shed stank of weed killer and of the armor's pungent smell of frying fat.

The sight of the giant wasp standing inert in the corner repulsed Ethan. The black striped patterns on the gold exoskeleton rippled and morphed to blend with the shadows.

Geez—a *tiny* wasp usually made him jump. This thing made Ethan want to scream.

He found that his hand, though, on its own, had reached out to touch it.

Creepy.

He curled his hand back.

Ethan promised himself he'd never get near one of these things again.

Dizzy and dazed, he tossed a plastic tarp over the insect and left it there. What else could he have done?

Ethan staggered home down the deserted streets. He snuck in the back door (miraculously without waking anyone up), and although he'd planned to get his parents and tell them everything, he changed into his pj's and climbed into his bed . . . just to rest for a few minutes.

Which is when his brain must have shut down and pushed these memories into some deep, dark corner.

And the bruises covering his body this morning?

He'd gotten those from fighting giant robots, flying around at crazy speeds, and his less-than-perfect landing.

Maybe Ethan shouldn't trust his memory. It could have been a nightmare.

But the parka in his hands, that was real—which meant

being kidnapped by Felix and Madison had really happened, too.

His thoughts smashed to a stop.

If Felix and Madison's story about alien invasion and people being mentally absorbed was true . . . it meant *everything* in his neighborhood was a lie. Emma wasn't going off to Vassar Prep tomorrow! She was going someplace where the Ch'zar would take over her mind.

He had to warn her. Stop her.

Ethan tossed the parka and ran down the stairs three at a time.

He skidded to a halt in the dining room.

His parents, Franklin and Melinda Blackwood, sat at the table. Dad wore a black suit and tie. Mom had on the navy blue dress that she saved for formal parties.

Although the dining table had platters of pancakes and bacon, syrup and jams, stacks of toast, and a pitcher of juice, the plates before his parents, even their coffee cups, were empty.

As if they'd been sitting there waiting for him.

Ethan's dad looked serious. Sometimes people mistakenly thought he was serious because of his strong Cherokee jaw. This morning, though, his dark eyes looked deadly.

Mom smiled at him, but Ethan recognized it as her nervous smile.

She'd had on that same wavering smile when she'd stood in front of the School Board of Ethical Behaviors and explained how shooting off his model rockets into the neighbor's garage (and almost burning that house down) had been a stupid accident.

These were his parents—the ones who'd cheered him on at every soccer match, bandaged his scrapes, tucked him into bed when he was a little kid. Parents who loved him—weren't they?

How could Franklin and Melinda Blackwood be mentally controlled by aliens?

It seemed impossible.

"Where's Emma?" Ethan asked, growing concerned.

"We sent her out into the driveway to wait," his mom said, and glanced out the curtained window.

"It's to give us time to talk." Dad set his large hands on the table in what looked like a normal, relaxed gesture . . . if not for his fingers turning white from how hard he pressed down.

"Sit, honey." Mom pulled out the chair next to her.

Ethan took a step back. "I'll stand."

His parents looked startled at his disobedience. Ethan *always* did as he was told.

His dad's hands relaxed. "Listen, Ethan," he said. "We know what happened last night."

Ethan stopped breathing.

Were they saying they knew about the fight on the mountain? Were they saying they knew *he* knew about the Ch'zar?

What would the Ethan Blackwood who was supposed to know nothing about the real outside world tell his maybe-mind-controlled parents?

Ethan slowly exhaled and tried to slow his racing pulse. "Yeah . . . sorry about not getting the trash off the lawn," he said. "Just don't ground me—or if you're going to, please do it after state finals. The team needs me."

Mom continued to smile, but somehow it looked like she was about to cry, too.

"That was good," Dad whispered, leaning forward. "Very good, Ethan. Not so much a lie, but not giving away any real information, either. Remember that. It will come in handy."

Ethan stood perfectly still, shocked, trying to understand what his dad had said.

Had he just given him advice on how to *lie*?

"You know?" Ethan whispered. "Everything?"

"Shhh," his mother said. She wasn't smiling anymore.

"We knew this day would come," Dad said. He looked suddenly weak and helpless.

"But it wasn't supposed to happen," Mom said, turning to his father. "Not Ethan first. It was supposed to be Emma—"

Dad set a hand on hers and she fell quiet.

Ethan wanted to run to his mom, hug her, but he didn't even know if she *was* his mom anymore.

Or if she had *ever* really been his mom.

"We've done everything we could to get you and

Emma ready," Dad said. "We can't tell you more, Ethan. We don't know how this will end. If it goes bad . . . then you can't know." He looked away, unable to meet Ethan's eyes. "And if it goes well, then you'll understand. Maybe you'll even forgive us one day."

"Remember what we've taught you," Mom whispered. There was a hitch in her voice. "Not just what we're *supposed* to have taught you, but everything else that makes you a Blackwood. You and Emma aren't like anyone else here. You're smarter. Tougher. And you're able to think for yourselves."

Ethan didn't understand.

He knew what he felt, though—confused, lonely, and very scared.

He couldn't stand it anymore. He *had to* tell them everything that had happened. He didn't care if they were controlled by the Ch'zar.

They were his parents. They had to understand. They *had to* really love him.

Before he could say anything, Ethan heard his sister stomp up the porch steps (making much more noise than she usually did with her big feet).

The front door opened.

Coach Norman was with Emma.

Behind him were two police officers.

"Ethan," Coach Norman said. He looked relieved to see him. "I'm so glad you're safe."

Ethan turned to his parents, hoping they'd get up and

stand next to him—just like they both had when he'd been in real trouble before.

He had a very bad feeling about Coach and those policemen.

His mom and dad sat there with no expression . . . then his dad gave him the slightest, almost invisible shake of his head.

"There's been some vandalism at the school," one of the police officers said. "We'd like you to come with us."

"Just to answer a few questions," the second officer added. He smiled, but it wasn't friendly.

Ethan's knees wobbled.

Coach Norman crossed the room, took Ethan by the elbow, and steadied him. "Don't worry, Blackwood. Everything's going to be okay."

But for the first time in his life, Ethan knew that Coach Norman was lying to him.

∘ ∘ ∘ 9 ∘ ∘ ∘

PIECES OF TRUTH

"THIS WILL JUST TAKE A MINUTE, BLACKWOOD."
Coach sat at his desk and laid out a photocopy of Ethan's
school file. He ran one hand over his silver buzz-cut hair
and then leafed through the pages.

Ethan fidgeted in a metal folding chair.

The police had escorted him to Coach's office. Every
time Ethan had come here—for routine counseling or to
talk soccer strategy or even if Coach was telling him he'd
done a good job—Ethan had always felt awkward and
small.

It was because of the Wall.

Coach's office had a big window that looked out onto
the practice field, a huge desk in the center, and a metal
chair for a visitor.

When you sat in it, you had to face the wall behind
his desk.

The Wall had shelves crammed with trophies from soccer matches, basketball tournaments, and track races, and gold-plated footballs. Because Coach was also guidance counselor for half the students at Northside Elementary, there were framed pictures of spelling bee finalists and scholarship recipients, too.

Hundreds of Northside champions and winners looked down at Ethan.

Ethan always felt like he was letting them down.

Today it felt worse—because for the first time in his life, he knew the truth. Those champion students hadn't gone on to high school to study and make the world a better place, or become sports superstars or astronauts.

What did the Ch'zar do with them all?

Ethan turned and tried to smile at the two police officers guarding the door.

Their hands moved to their billy clubs.

Officer Grace, the older of the two, had a salt-and-pepper mustache. Officer Hendrix had freckles and red hair. The two had come to school once to give a lecture on fire safety. Ethan had never heard of anyone getting into enough trouble to be brought in for questioning by them . . . until today, that is.

He wanted to think everything Felix and Madison had told him was a lie. Or that this was all a bad dream.

Ethan was way beyond that now.

His gaze settled on Coach Norman. So how did he fit into all this?

He'd always been there for Ethan, not exactly a friend but someone who (Ethan had thought) had his well-being in mind . . . and had good advice for him.

Superior long-range strategy always wins over superior immediate tactics.

What was Ethan's long-range strategy? Surrender to aliens who'd take his mind? No way!

"Well, Blackwood," Coach said, and looked at Ethan. "We still playing games? Or should we try the truth?"

Ethan gulped. He wasn't sure what to say. As with his parents, Ethan wanted to believe that Coach couldn't be part of the Ch'zar's plans.

He whispered, "The truth, Coach." Ethan mustered his courage and asked, "Were the soccer matches at least real?"

Coach Norman smiled. "They were real," he said. "It's an effective way to isolate potential leaders from the group. We keep a careful eye on leader types. They can be trouble."

"Like me?"

"Very much like you." Coach's smile vanished. "I want you to tell me everything that happened last night. Start when you were abducted by the Resisters."

Ethan's cheeks flushed.

How did Coach know about them? Ch'zar Collective mind or not . . . no one had seen Ethan.

"I don't know what you're talking about," Ethan said.

Coach took out photos from Ethan's school record. He spread them on the desk.

Ethan picked one up. It was a grainy black-and-white picture. It showed Ethan and Emma outside their house right after the party last night.

The next picture was of Ethan alone, kicking a paper cup at the recycle bin. He looked angry . . . and it was obvious he'd missed the shot. How embarrassing.

In the next photo was the milk truck . . . and the one after that showed Felix and Madison getting out. Ethan noted Madison had jumped out before the truck stopped and sneaked through the shadows behind him—that was how she'd surprised him.

In the last picture, Felix shoved a blurred Ethan into the truck.

"We have more pictures of the milk truck driving through town," Coach said. "Out on Avenue K. And then we lost it when it entered the national forest."

Ethan's mouth dropped open.

Who took all these pictures? Why would anyone watch *him* in the first place?

"Automatic cameras," Coach explained. "We see everything. All the time. Even—"

He set down two more pictures.

One had Northside students on the dance floor. It was last week's Sadie Hawkins dance . . . and in one corner stood Ethan, holding Mary Vincent's hand.

He looked frightened. Well, he had been. He hadn't realized how much he'd looked like a complete dork.

He picked up the last picture.

It was his dining room at home. This morning. Ethan stood there talking to his parents.

Ethan's skin crawled. They were *always* watching.

Until this instant, he'd thought of Santa Blanca, his neighborhood, and most of all his home as safe places.

But that was backward.

He wasn't safe here. Ethan and Emma and all the kids were prisoners, watched twenty-four hours a day.

He'd been an idiot! The only time he'd been really free was with Felix and Madison . . . and he'd blown it, panicked, and run from them.

Ethan felt something curl up inside him and die.

Now Coach and the others had him trapped.

Okay, that might be true, but Ethan wouldn't help them. It was bad enough leaving Felix and Madison when they'd needed his help. Ethan wouldn't *add* to his mistake.

"I've got nothing to tell you," Ethan said.

"No?" Coach pulled open a drawer. He took out a finger-sized red crystal and set it on his chipped plastic desk. "Maybe we can convince you otherwise."

He snapped shut the blinds on his window.

The crystal flickered with light, and a hologram of the Earth popped into view, hovering a foot in the air.

It was like no computer display in school, like no computer *anywhere* that Ethan had ever seen or heard about.

The globe spun around and the view zoomed in.

"Fifty-seven years ago," Coach said, "the human race was doing its best to destroy itself in World War Four."

Dots of lightning appeared in the clouds over the Earth, then cooled into red mushrooms of fire. Huge swaths of the Amazon rain forest smoldered. Lasers made a web around the globe and popped satellites.

"Just when it looked hopeless," Coach whispered, "*they* came."

∘ ∘ ∘ 10 ∘ ∘ ∘

THEIR UNIVERSAL MESSAGE

THE HOLOGRAPHIC EARTH SHRANK AND Ethan saw the moon. A planetoid one-eighth the size of the moon emerged from its shadow.

Only this planetoid was artificial, with spikes and warts, vast plains of hexagonal patterns like part of a giant insect eye, and swarms of smaller satellites that circled it.

Ethan felt awe at the size of this spaceship . . . and every instinct he had made him scoot as far back as he could in the metal chair.

"They stopped the war," Coach told him. "Do you know how?"

"They conquered us?"

Coach laughed. "No. The only thing they did was let us speak to each other for the first time in history. Men and women, those from the east and the west, the north and the south, all races, all colors, all religions—we finally *understood* one another."

Coach Norman leaned in so close, his face glowed from the holographic moonlight. "In an instant, all the misunderstanding and hatred melted away. We became brothers and sisters."

He waved his hands in frustration, trying to explain something that Ethan guessed couldn't be explained but could only be experienced.

That had to be the Ch'zar Collective mind control.

Hadn't Madison said it gave them all some sort of telepathy, too?

"*What* are they?" Ethan whispered, his curiosity temporarily winning out over how weird and scary this situation was. "The Ch'zar, I mean. Are they giant insects?"

Coach chuckled. "No human has seen them. They live in the mothership in orbit." He tapped the side of his head. "Only if you join can you see them and understand what they are."

So . . . Coach must no longer think he was human. That was creepy.

"But it's not mental domination," Coach said. "I bet that's what the Resisters told you. Almost everyone on the planet *willingly* joined and worked together for the common good."

"I've seen what 'working together for the common good' looks like," Ethan said. "Building-sized robots stripmining the planet!"

"You saw one of our most productive titanium fields. A necessary operation."

On Coach's desk appeared holographic forests and fields of wildflowers in full bloom.

"But the Collective has also restored the rain forests," Coach told him, "neutralized radiation across the world, and made the Sahara Desert a lush grassland preserve."

Ethan was confused now.

He knew what he'd seen on the mountaintop with Felix and Madison . . . but that didn't mean this other side of the Ch'zar story couldn't be true too.

"We've built things humanity could never have done alone," Coach said. "Elevators that reach orbit altitude and spaceship probes that we've sent to explore the nearby stars."

The holographic images morphed into the alien mothership. Also in orbit about the moon were three other, incomplete copies of that original ship.

"And soon we'll all go to the stars," Coach explained. "The Ch'zar Collective has fourteen other alien species who joined before they found us. We work together for the good of each other in harmony—for peaceful purposes."

"So you're all about peace?" Ethan asked, and crossed his arms over his chest. "Then why were you trying to *kill us* on top of that mountain?"

Coach waved his hands as if to brush Ethan's argument aside. "Even though the Resisters have caused untold damage and threaten everything we've built . . . we're just trying to capture them. All life is precious to us. Even our enemies' lives."

"You were shooting stingers at us the size of my arm!" Ethan protested.

"Oh, I'll admit they look scary. But if they'd hit you, they would have pumped you full of a tranquilizer and put you to sleep. That's it."

It was true that the Ch'zar had only started firing lasers at them once they were in the fighting suits. Could they have just been trying to capture them?

"What about the robots that tore the mountain apart to get us? One of them almost smashed me flat."

Coach snorted. "A direct hit inside one of those fighting suits would have barely knocked you down."

Ethan recalled how easily he'd caught the fist of one of those monster robots—and how easily he'd tossed it aside.

"I know you're confused, son," Coach said. He stood and came around to Ethan's side of the desk. "But we're the good guys here. You've got to tell us . . . where did you hide the fighting suit?"

The good guys? Ethan almost laughed.

He was a long, long way from trusting anything Coach said . . . and yet pieces of his story seemed to fit.

Could *some* of it be the truth?

One thing *didn't* make sense, though.

"I thought you guys had cameras everywhere," Ethan said. "Didn't you *see* the wasp suit?" He made a fumbling gesture at the closed window and the soccer field beyond. "And my crash landing?"

"We tracked your trajectory into the valley," Coach said, and sat on his desk, distorting the hologram. "But getting an *exact* position with radar was impossible because the suit has an active stealth technology we don't yet understand."

How could Madison and Felix have technology *more* advanced than the Ch'zar? There was an important piece of the human-Ch'zar story still missing.

"Then your 'wasp,' as you call it," Coach continued, "dropped low into Santa Blanca, and its antielectronic systems jammed every camera within a mile of the school."

"That must have been inconvenient," Ethan said.

His sarcasm was a shock. Ethan had been raised never to talk back to adults. This once, though, it kind of felt good.

Coach's rugged face froze for a split second, and then he frowned.

Then it sank in what Coach had just told him . . . and what it meant.

They *didn't* have the fighting suit.

If Ethan could somehow get to it, he could fly out of here—to where, he wasn't sure, but it would give him time to think and come up with a plan.

"What's so important about that suit?" Ethan asked. "They said they stole it from *you*—maybe they added a few things—that antielectronic whatsit. But the mighty Ch'zar Collective, fourteen alien races all working peacefully together for the common good . . . you guys have to have better technology than two kids. Don't you?"

More sarcasm. And this time Ethan was certain it felt good.

Coach's jaw set, and he ground his teeth. He leaned closer, his face an inch from Ethan's, and whispered, "Just tell us where the suit is, son." He leaned back and exhaled. "Do the right thing. Help us bring these criminals to justice."

Do the right thing.

Ethan opened his mouth and started to tell Coach where he'd stashed the suit.

He realized that "doing the right thing" was a knee-jerk involuntary reaction—what he'd been taught to do for the last twelve years by his teachers and every book he'd read in Santa Blanca.

But Ethan had also been raised by Franklin and Melinda Blackwood, who'd taught him to think for himself.

And while he was thinking for himself, another very important fact clicked in his brain.

"You didn't get them—Madison and Felix got away. If they hadn't . . . you'd have *their* suits and you wouldn't need the wasp."

Coach went back to his side of the desk without comment.

Ethan was relieved that Felix and Madison hadn't been captured or killed. Leaving a fight was a mistake he'd never make again, if he got the chance. Coach Norman closed Ethan's file. He got out a rubber stamp and blew the dust off it.

"Please, Ethan," he said. "One way or another we *will* get what we need out of you. In the end, you'll see the Ch'zar Collective is the best thing that ever happened to the human race."

"I don't think so," Ethan said. "You know why?"

"Tell me, son."

"Because the Ch'zar don't *ask* if anyone wants to join. If the truth was really so great, you'd give us kids a choice. You wouldn't have to lie."

Coach pinched the bridge of his nose and replied, "Would you give a baby a choice to get a life-saving vaccination?"

He jotted a few notes on Ethan's file folder:

CAUTION—high intellectual potential
Confirmed leader type
Irrevocable contamination

Coach rubber-stamped it with large red letters: SRS.

"I'm sorry, Ethan," he said. "We'll get your willing co-operation, whatever that takes."

"SRS . . . ," Ethan whispered. He had a sinking feeling about those three letters.

"Sterling Reform School," Coach told him.

Reform school was for criminals and kids who went crazy. Ethan had never known anyone bad enough to go . . . although he'd heard stories. Reform school had forced labor and remedial training, and no one ever got into a good high school after reform school.

He caught himself. What was he thinking? Why worry about high school now? That was just another lie.

He had to get out of here!

Ethan stood, knocking over the metal chair.

Officers Grace and Hendrix grabbed him from behind.

He struggled, but they were too strong.

"It won't be that bad," Coach assured him. "A couple of injections of growth hormone and a few other chemicals will trigger puberty for you in a matter of hours instead of months. We would've preferred to have you fully developed before you understood the Ch'zar's universal message—but this will have to do."

Ethan kicked and screamed, but they dragged him off.

"Don't worry, son," Coach said as he filed Ethan's record. "Soon you'll understand . . . like the rest of us."

○ ○ ○ **11** ○ ○ ○

PRISONER BUS RIDE

OFFICERS GRACE AND HENDRIX ESCORTED Ethan into the hallway.

Any ideas he had about making a break for it died the instant he stepped outside. Every Northside teacher and janitor was in the hall making sure students didn't enter the central corridor.

The adults turned at the same time to look at Ethan— all staring at him with unblinking eyes.

Ethan had seen that look before. Bottomless. Unreadable. It was the same look in the segmented eyes of the giant wasp when it had first noticed him.

The adults went back, holding up their hands and telling everyone that this hall had to be kept clear for five more minutes. It was an "emergency drill." There was "nothing to worry about." And the kids were told to "move along to your classes."

Ethan spied his soccer teammate Bobby walking from first-period English to second-period pre-algebra. Mary Vincent was with him. They were talking and laughing. Neither saw Ethan.

What were *they* doing together?

He jerked toward them and opened his mouth to shout.

Officer Grace pulled him back. "Not a word, Blackwood," he whispered. "Contaminate any of these others and we'll ship them off with you."

Ethan considered.

For a moment he imagined he'd tell everyone what was going on—yell it out—and all the kids would join and rise up against the mind-controlled adults. . . .

But that's not what he did.

If he started shouting the truth, he'd get dragged off, probably hurt in the process, and he'd definitely get Bobby and Mary into trouble with him.

Plus . . . who'd believe him?

He barely believed any of this, and he'd seen the Ch'zar firsthand.

He hung his head and reluctantly let himself get pushed along by the police. A half-dozen adults went with them to make sure there was no problem.

Ethan wondered if Coach Norman had been an A student and all-star athlete too. Raised in a neighborhood just like this, he probably thought he'd go to high school . . . then he hit puberty . . . his brain changed . . . the Ch'zar got inside . . . and they had him.

The real Coach Norman must have died that day.

They took Ethan to the garage and guided him to a black bus. Ethan had never seen this particular bus before. Stenciled on the side of it in silver letters was: THE STERLING SCHOOL.

Sterling. The place was legendary. Notorious.

It was where the criminals and antisocial types were sent. The troublemakers. Like Ethan Blackwood.

There'd be no sports scholarship, no MIT, no learning from the best science teachers and one day becoming an astronaut. He felt a stab of regret.

But those dreams had never been real.

At least now he knew the truth . . . for all the good it did him.

Officers Grace and Hendrix marched him onto the bus. There were no chains or shackles inside, as Ethan had expected. Instead, it was like any other bus he'd been on, with rows of side-by-side padded seats, overhead video monitors, and the faint scent of bubble gum.

They gave Ethan a shove and indicated he should go all the way to the back.

The seat belts weren't the standard lap variety. They were five-point harnesses—probably designed to prevent the passengers—or rather the *prisoners*—from escaping.

Ethan couldn't be here. He had to get off this bus. Now! It'd be his last chance to escape.

He stopped and tried to turn—but the police grabbed him and forced him into a seat.

Ethan struggled and screamed.

The two officers were strong and seemingly impervious to his punches and kicks.

They wrestled him into a window seat and snapped his harness in place.

"You'll see this is all for the best," Officer Grace told him.

"Just relax, boy," Officer Hendrix soothed. "It'll be easier."

"I bet it'll be easier," Ethan said, "for you!"

He wriggled and strained, clutched at the release button on his safety harness—but, of course, it didn't work.

The police officers looked at each other and shook their heads, as if Ethan was a terrible disappointment. They got off the bus.

The folding doors sealed with a swish, and the bus on full autopilot pulled out of the garage.

It cruised through his neighborhood and turned onto Main Street. Was this the last time Ethan would see his home? There was the drugstore on the corner where he and Emma went to listen to the mystery radio shows every Saturday afternoon. Looking over the downtown rooftops, he thought he caught a glimpse of blue and white—the peak of his house.

Ethan hugged his stomach and felt like he was going to be sick.

Were his parents like Coach Norman? Part of the alien Collective? Had they ever loved him? Or was that an act?

No. Franklin and Melinda Blackwood *were* different.

Everyone had always said so. Hadn't they taught him and Emma to think for themselves? That didn't seem to fit into being a good citizen of the Collective.

And what had they told him at breakfast?

We've done everything we could to get you and Emma ready. We don't know how this will end. If it goes bad . . . then you can't know.

Which made sense only if his parents *weren't* controlled by the aliens—and they'd been trying to hide that from him! They'd have had to, because if Ethan got absorbed into the Collective . . . then the Ch'zar would know everything he did.

Maybe his parents were secret Resistance spies. They were just waiting for the right moment to rescue him before he changed into a mind-controlled zombie.

His heart sank. Did that now mean the Ch'zar, when they absorbed Ethan's mind, would suspect his parents as well because he did? Had he blown it for them?

Ethan strained against his harness, looking out every window, waiting to catch a glimpse of his family's station wagon racing down the street after the bus.

But that didn't happen.

The bus turned off Main Street. Straight ahead was the Geo-Transit Tunnel that had a four-lane road and railroad tracks—the only way into and out of the mountain valley that held Santa Blanca.

It looked like a huge mouth about to swallow the bus and Ethan.

No one would swoop in at the last moment and save him.

Ethan arched his back, pulling his arms and legs once more against the restraints.

There was no way he was letting anyone take him away from his home! There was no way he was letting them take his mind!

His struggles just tightened the seat harness.

He slumped, exhausted.

The bus entered the tunnel, and darkness filled the bus.

"Welcome to the Sterling School for the Gifted," said a friendly girl's voice.

He blinked back brimming tears. Video screens lowered from the bus's ceiling. On-screen was a redheaded girl in a crisp black school uniform. She walked down an ivy-covered corridor.

"You're special!" the girl said. "And at Sterling, we know exactly how to put your special abilities to use."

She smiled, and the scene dissolved to a chemistry lab where boys and girls set beakers of boiling goo behind clear blast shields and watched the stuff explode.

What was this? They would *never* let him do that at Northside.

The girl in the video laughed. "We know you're inquisitive and creative, and maybe you even got punished because you were 'different.'"

The scene cut to a field full of boys and girls in black sweats who sparred with padded sticks. They seemed to be having a great time beating the snot out of each other.

Ethan gaped at the mass roughhousing. This stuff was totally frowned upon at Northside. Why make them aggressive *on purpose*?

"We're going to channel your natural leadership ability and make you stronger."

That was a lie.

Ethan figured it was to keep these "troublemaker" students busy until they hit puberty. Keep them from finding out the truth and escaping.

"We're proud of our Sterling graduates," the girl continued. "They go on to become senators—judges—policemen—and the leaders in *your* community!"

"More lies," Ethan said.

He balled his hands into fists.

The bus emerged from the tunnel, and the sudden sunlight made him blink. Through the windows he saw wheat fields waving in a breeze, windmills spinning to make clean energy, and a fruit stand selling apples.

"It's all lies!" He pounded his fist on the window—once, twice, three times.

The video presentation stopped.

A computer voice crackled through the speakers: *"Please do not damage Sterling School property. Demerits will be awarded. This is your only warning!"*

Ethan laughed. They thought demerits or detention were going to scare him *now*?

"You want to give demerits for something? Try this!"

He laced his hands and hammered them—right in the

middle of the window—again and again—once more . . . and a hairline crack splintered.

It was weird. That crack was white and red against the green fields.

Just as Ethan *knew* it had to be . . . because it wasn't a real window. It was a computer monitor, showing him what they wanted him to see.

He moved closer and looked through the crack.

He saw the *real* outside. It was dusty and red and gray, and the sun blazed overhead. Huge machines rumbled in the distance chewing through the mountains.

At least he knew he wasn't crazy.

He glared up at the speakers. "You can't stop me from knowing the truth."

Ethan heard a gentle hiss from the air-conditioning vents and smelled a faint chemical odor.

His heart raced.

Like Felix had told him, they were going to drug him.

While he was asleep, would they inject him with those chemicals that'd make him reach puberty faster? When he woke up . . . would he even be Ethan Blackwood anymore?

He turned back to the window and hammered over and over.

The single tiny crack resisted his efforts.

A tingling spread over Ethan's throat. He got dizzy.

This was it.

They were going to win.

Ethan mustered all his strength, tensed his entire body—and hit the window with everything he had.

A second crack splintered out from the first.

He'd done it.

But it was too late. The cracked window held.

His eyelids drooped . . . and closed.

Ethan jerked upright. No! He couldn't fall asleep!

He raised a trembling hand but felt his strength draining away.

He hit the glass.

Every window on his side of the bus shattered. Glass pebbles showered over Ethan. The bus shuddered and skidded to the side of the road. Hot wind, dust, and smoke blasted inside.

The chemical smell was gone, though.

Just in time. His head cleared.

Ethan stared at his hand . . . and then at the massive damage done to the bus.

There was no way *he* could've done this, was there?

A second impact sent the bus tumbling sideways.

It flipped—the other windows crumbled—metal wrenched and sparked.

Ethan, strapped upside down and helpless in his seat, tasted blood.

∘ ∘ ∘ 12 ∘ ∘ ∘

RESCUE PARTY

BLOOD RAN OUT OF ETHAN'S NOSE AND dripped to the floor—or rather the ceiling that was now where the floor should be in the overturned bus.

He coughed. The smoke got thicker.

What had just happened? Nothing made sense.

Maybe it was because he was hanging upside down, semidrugged and shaken.

From the back of the bus there was a sputtering and a sudden strong acrid odor. The battery packs were back there. From his chemistry class Ethan knew that if they cracked, they could leak an explosive gas.

He'd figure out what had happened to the bus later. He had to get out first!

The harness that had saved him from serious injury when the bus flipped was snug . . . and still locked.

He'd have to cut himself out. With what? The shattered glass was the "safe" kind, plastic-coated, that made tiny pebbles when it broke. He couldn't use it.

Under the seat ahead, though, a metal brace had twisted free and dangled there.

Ethan stretched—barely touched it with his fingertips, pulled it closer, grasped it, and pulled it free!

The end of the brace had a wicked, razor-sharp edge. Ethan sawed through the straps of his harness—and dropped headfirst onto the ceiling of the bus.

He scrambled out of a broken window and staggered from the bus.

The back of the bus had been crumpled like an empty aluminum can. Jets of gas spewed out.

Ethan ran up a nearby hill, climbing to the paved road the bus had been on.

The bus exploded! A wave of force and heat knocked him over. Flames shot through the passenger section and lifted the bus into the air—then it landed with a terrific crash.

A few seconds slower and Ethan would've been roasted alive.

He trembled but forced himself to stop, got to his feet, and got his bearings.

He was outside in the real world. It looked like a cross between the Sahara Desert and the cratered surface of the moon. There was no vegetation. The ground was a series of strip mines and toxic waste channels. The air was choked with dust . . . and drones.

A dozen of the same part-insect, part-rocket things that had attacked him yesterday circled the blackened, smoking remains of the school bus.

Three drones peeled off and landed, surrounding Ethan.

They were bigger than he remembered. Their slim torpedo bodies were about his size. Their wings were superthin translucent silver metal. Each had a single eye, a segmented bulb in which Ethan saw hundreds of hexagonal reflections of himself.

Their stingers pointed at him. They retracted with a click, like they were about to shoot.

The skin at the base of Ethan's spine crawled.

He tensed, trying to figure out how to dodge *three* of those darts at once.

A shadow streaked overhead—there was a hypersonic buzz—three red lights strobed so bright, they left Ethan blinking—and there were three flashes of heat that instantly sunburned his right arm.

The three drones around him sizzled, and lines of molten metal scarred their lengths. Their tiny insect legs gave out, and they dropped to the ground, inert.

Ethan's vision cleared and he saw a giant dragonfly zip between the drones over the bus, shooting them with lasers and ripping the closest to shrapnel with its front pincers.

"Madison!" He shouted and whooped for joy.

Ethan had never been so glad to see a bug before.

Thrumming filled the air behind him. Ethan turned, and a fifteen-foot-tall rhinoceros beetle dropped from the air three paces from him with enough force to make the earth tremble.

It was a terrifying sight . . . so much destructive armored force, so close.

The beetle's stubby black wings folded under its shell like Japanese origami.

"I *really* hope that's you, Felix," Ethan said.

The beetle took a menacing step closer.

Ethan felt absolute, life-threatening danger emanating from the thing, and he backed away.

Was Felix angry at him? Going to pulverize him because Ethan had ditched them yesterday? He had every right to be mad. Ethan's running away could have gotten them captured or killed . . . but if they were so angry, why come back and save him?

Was this even Felix? It could be some *other* combat beetle, controlled by the Ch'zar.

The beetle's horns flickered with blue beams that intersected and combined.

Ethan held up his hands in the universal gesture of peace and surrender. There was nowhere to hide. That particle beam would blast him into atoms!

Ethan heard and then felt a buzzing—a split second before he got sideswiped by an unstoppable force.

The dragonfly swooped in, yanked him off his feet, and soared into the air so quickly, the acceleration almost pulled the skin off his face.

He tried to scream but was going too fast to take a breath.

The dragonfly rolled and dove to the ground. It hovered to a stop so quickly that Ethan's stomach rattled in his rib cage.

The dragonfly unceremoniously dropped him on the dirt and took off into the air.

Dizzy, Ethan turned on wobbly legs and saw the beetle that had almost blasted him.

He was wrong, though. He hadn't been the beetle's target.

It crouched and blasted the ground—boiling dirt and stone into a fiery cauldron.

A pair of hooked insect jaws slashed at the beetle from where they'd been hidden underground.

Another bug.

Ethan recognized it. It was an ant lion—fat body, tiny head, and oversized jaws. He'd seen them before at the bottom of sandy pits, waiting for smaller bugs to wander by and fall in. Then they'd grab, crush, and devour whatever they sank their jaws into.

Only the ant lions Ethan had seen weren't the size of an eighteen-wheel truck, with armored jaws that looked like they could crush solid steel. They weren't covered in a thick silver armor that looked impenetrable. And any ant lion Ethan had seen before *definitely* didn't have a cannon mounted on its back!

Felix kept blasting the thing with his particle beam.

Madison shot down the remaining drones, and then her dragonfly strafed the ant lion with laser fire.

Their beams heated a section of the ant lion's silver armor. It sparkled and harmlessly reflected the energy.

The ant lion lunged at the rhinoceros beetle.

Felix jumped back, narrowly escaping the snap of its slashing jaws.

Where had that thing come from? Ethan couldn't figure out how it could have just been sitting there waiting for them.

More important, though: How were Felix and Madison going to kill it?

Missile launchers popped out from the sides of the rhinoceros beetle, and a pair of rockets whooshed out, struck the ant lion, and exploded in a thunderous cloud.

The ant lion was unfazed. It jumped and knocked Felix to the ground.

The rhinoceros beetle grappled and shoved the ant lion's cannon to one side just as it fired.

The ground exploded and sent both creatures tumbling into the air.

The beetle landed on its back, legs wriggling in a struggle to right itself.

The ant lion landed on its legs and scrambled toward Felix.

Ethan didn't think. He just knew he had to somehow stop that thing from ripping Felix apart.

Ethan owed him.

He picked up a fist-sized chunk of rock and hucked it as hard as he could.

It amazingly hit (and then not-so-amazingly bounced off) the ant lion. It didn't do any damage, but silver sensor hairs on the thing's armor rippled with irritation. It hesitated.

"Hey, shiny!" Ethan yelled. "You looking for me?"

It stopped. Its antennae twitched.

"Yeah, I'm talking to you! I've seen balls of tinfoil that looked scarier!"

The ant lion spun around, and its cannon aimed at Ethan.

"Uh-oh," Ethan whispered.

The problem with his not-thinking-ahead plan suddenly became very clear to him.

Madison's dragonfly swooped across the ant lion's path. It tracked her for a moment, then reoriented on Ethan.

Ethan couldn't think of anything to do.

He shook. . . .

No, it wasn't him. The ground *under* his feet trembled.

Felix's beetle had gotten up and was behind the ant lion, running, building speed, shaking the earth with its massive bulk. It leaped into the air and onto the ant lion's back!

The beetle used one horn to gore the seam where the cannon attached to the ant lion's armor.

The ant lion turned and tried to flip the huge rhinoceros beetle off, but it couldn't shake him.

Felix levered the gun up, exposing a crack in the ant lion's armor—and then fired his missiles into the breach.

Explosions and smoke and lightning filled the air . . . as well as chunks of silver armor and bug legs and the ant lion's jagged jaws, which went spinning over Ethan's head.

When the air cleared, the rhinoceros beetle lay in the center of a charred crater covered with green goo . . . not moving.

"Felix!" Ethan ran to him.

Madison's dragonfly landed nearby, its armor popped open, and she slid out.

The pattern on her bodysuit exactly matched the dragonfly's markings, but then the colors on her suit faded. Madison was drenched in sweat. Her normally spiked hair was plastered to her forehead.

She touched three different places on the beetle armor. The armor slid apart, revealing Felix inside, unconscious . . . or dead.

The big guy for once looked tiny inside the even larger monster insect fighting suit. Felix's face was perfectly still and peaceful.

A lump caught in Ethan's throat. "He's okay, isn't he?" Ethan whispered.

Madison ignored him and felt for a pulse on Felix's neck. She looked grim and rummaged through a small pouch on her belt, pulling out what looked like a Band-Aid. She peeled it and smoothed it onto Felix's neck.

After a moment Felix inhaled and looked around. "Did we win?" he whispered.

Madison looked like she was going to cry with happiness. "That was so stupid." She hugged Felix.

She helped him out of the fighting suit.

"Wow," Ethan said, breathless. "I don't even know how to—"

Madison whirled, grabbed Ethan by his shirt, and drew back her fist.

He'd never seen any person look like she did—like she wanted to knock his head off!

"I don't want to hear anything from you, Blackwood . . . ," she growled, "except where you stashed *our* Infiltrator I.C.E. fighting suit."

∘ ∘ ∘ 13 ∘ ∘ ∘

GOING BACK IN

THE BARN SMELLED OF FRESH HAY AND gasoline. It was an old place on the very edge of Blanca Dairy farmland. There was a rusted plow inside from when horses worked the fields.

Also under the hayloft stood two gigantic insects: a dragonfly and a rhinoceros beetle.

Felix tossed pitchforks of hay down on them to hide the out-of-place creatures. His shaved head glistened with sweat from the work.

Madison stood before Ethan, rubbing goop into his hair and combing it so roughly that she tore some out.

"Ow! Go easy, would you?"

"You're lucky it's just your hair I'm ripping out, Black-wood," she muttered.

She looked him over. "Missed a spot." She squeezed

more gunk out of the tube and rubbed it onto the back of his head. "You're going to make a pretty blond," she said with a snort of amusement.

Camouflaging hair dye. It was part of their plan to sneak back and get the wasp fighting suit.

Once Ethan had told them he'd hidden the suit in his neighborhood, they'd grabbed him and flown away from the wrecked bus, up and over the mountains, zooming *through* the forest to hide from aerial surveillance, stopping and then moving at precisely timed intervals to avoid what Felix called the "satellite web"—and then they came to this abandoned barn.

They'd changed into school uniforms. They even had one for Ethan . . . obviously stolen property, because the name tag inside read: HAROLD SMIDES.

Had this uniform been for the third member of their team? The one they'd lost?

It was probably a bad idea to ask. It had been a sore point before with Madison . . . and the last thing Ethan wanted was to make her *more* angry.

"What is it?" Madison said. "You have the same stupid look as those dairy cows in the pasture." She took some hair gunk and applied it to her head, then drew her hair back into a ponytail.

"Nothing . . . except you called the wasp suit Infiltrator I.C.E.? What does *that* mean?"

Madison rolled her eyes as if everyone ought to know. "I.C.E.—Insectoid Combat Exoskeleton," she said. "The wasp is an Infiltrator model. It's got moderate armor and weapons systems, designed to penetrate enemy defenses quickly—accomplish whatever its mission is—and then get out just as quick. It's devastating in running combat but not meant for prolonged engagements."

Ethan nodded, understanding. The wasp was fast, nimble, strong, but it wasn't the fastest or the strongest. It was a little good at everything.

"Your suit? And Felix's?"

"My dragonfly . . ." Madison's voice changed, and she got a far-off look in her eyes. It reminded Ethan of how some girls sounded when they talked about horses. "She's Reconnaissance I.C.E. Light armor, light weapons, but capable of *supersonic* flight. No one can catch us once we're in the air."

She exhaled and looked normal again.

"Felix's beetle is a brute," she said. "Juggernaut I.C.E. It can barely fly, but it's designed for sustained combat, with the heaviest armor, beam weapons, bombs, and missiles, and so strong it could tear down a mountain if it had to."

Felix finished heaping hay over the giant insects, brushed his blue-black bodysuit free of the straw, and joined them.

"Suits secured," he told Madison. "I activated the proximity sensors. If any Ch'zar come within a mile, I've programmed the suits to return to base. If they can't . . . they have orders to self-destruct."

She flashed him a lethal glare. "Now we're risking *all*

our suits to get the wasp. Why? They're bound to have it by now."

"Do we have a choice?" Felix said. "If the Ch'zar get our technology, we lose the tiny edge we have in this fight . . . and there's that *other* reason I want the wasp back." He returned her glare a moment and then turned to Ethan. "So, where did you put it? And did the adults say anything about the suit before they shipped you out?"

"The last place I saw it was at the school," Ethan said. "In a shed. I can show you. It wasn't really hidden . . . just kind of covered with a tarp."

Madison made a disgusted sound.

Ethan was about to tell her that he'd done his best . . . considering he'd just crash-landed at two hundred miles an hour into solid titanium—when he remembered something Coach had said that didn't make sense.

"They don't have it," Ethan told them. "They *really* wanted me to tell them where I'd stashed it. Even a simple search would have turned it up, so I don't understand why. They said they weren't able to track it in the air, either . . . something about it having 'stealth technology.' Does that make any sense to you guys?"

Madison and Felix shared a quick look of astonishment.

"A lucky break . . . ," Madison whispered.

"One we need to take advantage of," Felix said. "Fast."

Felix marched out of the barn and to the nearby farmhouse. Ethan and Madison followed. He went to a green minivan in the driveway. He opened the driver's door and motioned for them to get inside.

Felix bent under the dash and fiddled with the wires.

They were stealing this? Ethan looked around. They were going to get caught!

But no one in the farmhouse noticed.

And maybe no one would. Stuff like stealing cars just didn't happen in Santa Blanca.

Ethan saw the obvious advantages any criminal would have in a place like this. It felt wrong.

"When an Infiltrator suit goes into stealth mode," Felix explained, still rummaging under the dash, "it blocks radar and scrambles the mental signals used by the Ch'zar. Kind of a mental static, not enough to harm anyone's brain, but it does make a blind spot. Mind-controlled people see the stealthed wasp but don't pay any attention to it."

"Doesn't work if you fly into a crowd of adults," Madison said. "Or if there are other kids around."

"Tonight they'll send in sensor bugs to sweep the area," Felix said.

"That only gives us an hour to get there and get out," Madison whispered, an edge of worry creeping into her voice.

Felix twisted wires together. The minivan started.

He put on his seat belt and asked Ethan, "What do you think? Is there time?"

Ethan was surprised. Felix was treating him like he was part of his team . . . and after all the trouble he'd caused.

More than trouble. Ethan had almost gotten Madison and Felix *killed*. Twice!

Of course, they hadn't exactly treated him fairly either—kidnapping him and forcing him up that mountain. But what else could they have done? He hadn't believed Madison when she had told him the truth.

And if they hadn't taken Ethan, in a few months he'd have hit puberty and been one more brainwashed Ch'zar slave.

But he wasn't the only one about to be absorbed into the Collective.

Emma! She was leaving tomorrow! He had to warn her.

One crisis at a time, though. Ethan didn't deserve a second chance, but he was getting it. He wasn't going to mess it up. He'd help Felix and Madison get their suit back, then he'd find his sister and figure out how to save her, too.

"Time's not the problem," Ethan told Felix. "It's a fifteen-minute drive. Getting into the school will be the tricky part."

"That's no problem," Madison replied. She let her hair down, smoothed out the spikes that had popped up, and almost looked like a normal pretty girl.

"We're just three students," she said. "Who's going to know the difference? Besides, if the Ch'zar know you escaped, the last place they'd be looking for you would be back at brainwashed-central elementary school."

Felix snugged a baseball cap over his shaved head.

Ethan didn't say anything.

Sure, they had school uniforms, and his hair was a different color . . . but Ethan had spotted Felix and Madison easily at that soccer game—superpale, Madison's wild eyes, their antisocial attitudes. No matter their disguise, those two just didn't fit in.

Felix pulled out of the driveway and sped down the road.

"Just one more thing bothers me, Ethan," Felix said. "How did you get away from the fight on the mountain? You vanished off my sensors. I'm not blaming you for freaking out. I'm astonished you got the wasp to move as well as you did. Most pilots don't do half as well on their first attempt."

Ethan shrugged. "It was an accident."

He explained how he'd unintentionally jumped off the cliff, how he had wished he wouldn't hit the ground and could fly like Madison—which was when the wasp's wings popped out.

He paused to consider that technically the fighting suit couldn't be a wasp, because a wasp's wings didn't fold under its carapace like a beetle's. Of course, if the Resisters could engineer a giant fighting insect suit, they could probably cut and slice enough DNA to make a wasp's wings fold under its exoskeleton.

Meanwhile, Madison's mouth dropped open. "You flew just by *thinking* about it?"

"That *would* explain how he got back to Santa Blanca

so fast," Felix whispered to her. "As improbable as it seems."

"It's the truth," Ethan said, feeling defensive.

They expected him to believe their story about alien invasion and mind control, and they couldn't cut him a little slack about flying the suit? "What's so weird about that? You guys fly."

"Forget it." Madison tried, and failed, to wipe the sneer off her face. "Beginner's luck."

Felix burned rubber, pushing the minivan as fast as it would go—then downshifted and screeched to the posted speed limit once they hit the neighborhood. He casually pulled into the Northside Elementary parking lot like he owned the place.

They got out and marched onto the campus.

Madison and Felix strolled down the hallway.

Ethan felt like he had a big red sign plastered to his back that read:

I'M THE ONE YOU'RE LOOKING FOR!!

But no students were here. The last class had let out ten minutes ago.

Ethan's heart stopped.

The principal and three adults in suits turned down a side corridor and walked straight toward them.

THE MISSION

ETHAN THOUGHT HE'D DIE. THE PRINCIPAL AND three adults in black suits and ties saw them. They had to.

He knew it'd attract attention, but Ethan couldn't look away.

He wondered if he should run for it . . . or, as impossible as it sounded to him, try to walk nonchalantly like he was off to some after-school drama rehearsal.

The adults didn't even glance at them and turned down another hallway.

"See?" Madison not-so-playfully bumped her shoulder into his (which sent him stumbling off balance). "When the Ch'zar makes up its collective mind—in this case that you've escaped—it takes a lot for them to change it."

"You mean you guys were gambling that's what they'd think?" Ethan whispered. "Couldn't they have just as easily decided I'd come back to get the suit? Set some huge trap?"

"It's a good gamble," Felix replied. "The Ch'zar think logically, and what we're doing . . . no one in their right mind would try it."

Madison narrowed her eyes, and her tone changed to dead serious as she asked Ethan, "Now where's the suit?"

Ethan led them past the new soccer field . . . which yesterday had been acres of smooth green titanium. Now it was crumpled metal ruins with an impact crease that looked like a meteor had struck.

"Whoa," Felix whispered. "*You* did that?"

Ethan flushed. "I got the flying part down okay," he said, "but I need help with my landings."

He led them past the field, around the gym, and to the campus heat plant. Nestled in the shadow of the larger building was the gardener's shed.

Ethan stopped, looked around, and made sure no one had followed them.

He opened the shed door, they all went in, and he closed it behind them.

The scent of weed killer was overwhelming.

"Here," Ethan said, and marched to the corner. He pulled off the plastic tarp.

The giant wasp was there.

He sighed with relief.

He couldn't believe that Coach had missed it in his search. Felix had to be right. He'd probably come here and taken a quick look, and that "blind spot" thing must've kicked in. Even though he had to have seen a huge lump covered with a tarp, he'd ignored it.

"Oh no!" Madison cried. She knelt by the insect.

The wasp was curled up on the floor and looked much like an insect you'd find on a windowsill . . . an insect *long dead*.

Ethan pressed his hand to his own chest, and he could almost feel the thing's too-slow heartbeat.

Madison touched the golden armor here and there, but it remained unmoving. "Hibernation mode," she told Felix.

Felix's mouth set into a grim frown and he shook his head. "We have to abort, then. I'll set the self-destruct for ten minutes. I want to be far out of town when it goes off."

"What are you talking about?" Ethan asked.

"No." Madison set her hand flat on the wasp's thorax. "We were so close . . . and this is all I have left of him."

"I'm sorry," Felix said to her. "I wanted his suit back as much as you did, but there's no choice. He would've wanted it this way. You know that."

She hung her head and pinched the bridge of her crooked nose. "He would have wanted the mission *finished*," she whispered, and her voice broke.

"But we found it," Ethan said, more confused than ever. "So it's in this 'hibernation mode' thing. Just wake it up. Or we drag it back to the minivan. If we ditch the back seats, we can stuff it inside."

"An unloaded Infiltrator suit weighs *three tons*," Felix said. "And even if we used this"—he gestured at the riding lawn mower—"it'd be slow and attract way too much attention."

"Once it's in hibernation," Madison said, now defeated, "it takes a team of technicians hours to wake an I.C.E. suit." She removed her hand from the insect, hesitating as if it physically hurt to part with it.

Ethan realized it wasn't just the suit she had to leave behind.

The suit had belonged to the lost third member of their team . . . someone who had obviously meant a lot to Madison.

He wasn't happy about destroying the suit either, but he understood Felix's point about keeping it from the Ch'zar.

Ethan was, in fact, itching to finish this, get to Emma, and warn her. He wanted to figure out if his parents were part of the creepy Collective, too.

And yet, seeing Madison on the verge of tears . . . he *had to* help her somehow.

Ethan marched to the wasp. He knelt next to it and pounded on it like he had when it had first opened for him.

"Get up!" he demanded.

"Don't . . . ," Madison said. "There's nothing anyone can do."

As his fist touched the armor, something clicked in his mind.

A connection.

It was like Ethan was dreaming and struggling, swimming upward through sleep to wakefulness . . . and when he finally opened his eyes, he stared at himself and Felix and Madison and saw every single tool and shelf in the shed . . . because he was looking through the compound eyes of the wasp.

He and the wasp stood.

Fluid pumped through his limbs, his vision filled with blinking status lights, and even the stinger-laser on his tail heated to standby mode. He felt strong enough to tear through the shed.

Ethan released the armor plates that covered the cockpit.

Now let me go, he thought. *And thanks for waking up.*

His mind detached from the wasp.

But part of the insect's mind clung to him. It was like a warm coat he'd put on to protect himself from the cold. It was like a friend. Like a part of himself that he didn't want to leave.

Was this what it would feel like being in the Ch'zar Collective? Only instead of joining with one, you'd be surrounded by millions and millions of minds. You'd feel totally safe. Perfectly welcome.

Completely lost.

He could drown in that feeling, lose the Ethan Blackwood that his parents had taught to be strong and make his own choices.

Ethan snapped out of it.

He found himself standing in the shed. Cold and alone.

But himself.

Madison and Felix stared dumbfounded at him.

"You can't do that," Madison whispered.

Felix snapped his thick fingers in front of Ethan's face. "Are you with us, Blackwood? You spaced out for a second."

"Sure. Why wouldn't I be?" he said.

"No one has ever force-started an I.C.E. from hibernation," Madison breathed. "He's a freak."

"Or a prodigy," Felix murmured.

Felix and Madison looked at each other.

Felix shook his head no at the same time Madison's face brightened and she nodded yes.

"It should be easy to get the suit out," Ethan said, obviously not in on their secret, silent conversation. "Right?"

"You can *really* fly it?" Madison asked. "Fight? Everything?"

"I did before," Ethan told her, "under a lot more pressure."

"Don't . . . ," Felix told Madison.

"But now we can complete the mission." Madison glanced at her watch. "We have twelve minutes. That's just enough time for Blackwood to fly us back to the barn. We get our suits and the three of us stop that train."

"Train?" Ethan said to himself.

How could he have forgotten? Emma and a half-dozen other students had been accepted into Early Honors Admission. That train would take Santa Blanca's best and brightest away—kids thinking they were about to start the rest of their lives, when in reality their lives as individual people were about to end.

"You know how important this mission is," Madison went on, almost pleading with Felix. "Santa Blanca is the train's *first* transfer. We stop it before it gets here, and it saves kids in nine other neighborhoods. We can throw the entire Ch'zar harvesting apparatus into chaos. Maybe retrieve some of the—"

"No," Felix said. "I'm in charge of this mission. We lost one member of the team already. We almost lost one of our suits. Twelve minutes isn't time enough for us to get back, scout the area, and set up a proper operation."

These two could argue all day, but Ethan had to do *something*. His sister's life was at stake.

He could go to her—assuming no adult found him, and also assuming he could convince her that he wasn't crazy—and he could stop her from getting on that train. But even if he could, that'd just delay the inevitable.

Emma was a year older than him. She'd change sooner. Become an adult . . . and be absorbed into the Collective no matter what he did.

He had to do something better. Bigger.

Like stop the Ch'zar.

In a soccer match, sometimes the field cleared of defenders all the way to the goal, and you took the shot.

Ethan saw this was the same thing. He was going to take his best shot.

He went to the wasp and put his legs into the creature. "I'm going," he told them. "My sister's supposed to get on that train. I'll do whatever it takes to stop it."

Felix grabbed his arm. "I can't let you do that."

Ethan stared at his grip. "Can you stop me?"

Their eyes met.

Felix didn't blink. Neither did Ethan.

Ethan knew the big guy could pull him out of the suit and knock him silly if he wanted, but something was different between the two of them now.

Standing inside the wasp suit, Ethan felt . . . not exactly invulnerable, but at least an equal match for powerful Felix.

Felix let go and tapped a few controls inside the wasp.

He turned back to Ethan and flashed him an angry look. "I *can* stop you," he whispered. "I'm not going to, though, because Madison's right. We were sent to stop that train—it's important to the Resistance—and we're going to do it. But we're going to do it *my* way, understand?"

Ethan nodded. He listened. He had a feeling his life might depend on what Felix told him next.

"I set your autopilot to turn on if you lose consciousness," Felix said. "It'll access the parts of your brain that regulate breathing and heartbeat to fly the suit back to our base. If the armor gets compromised, though, or if you die . . . then the suit will self-destruct. Do you understand?"

Ethan swallowed. "Yeah. Got it."

"Good. Fly over the mountains. Keep low. If you're not

spotted, watch the tunnel entrance. We'll meet you there. If you see the train, do *not* engage it. It'll be too heavily defended. Instead, fire on the train tracks. Blow those up, and it'll have to stop. That will give us time to get to you. Now, repeat that back to me."

"Fly over the mountains," Ethan said. "Watch the tunnel entrance. Shoot the tracks. Wait for you. I got it."

Felix set one of his hunormous hands on Ethan's shoulder and squeezed. "I'm not sure if you're brave or monumentally stupid like Madison says, but either way, Ethan, good luck. We'll catch up as soon as we can."

Ethan felt like he was going to be sick, but he had to hold it together a little longer . . . for his sister.

"Thanks," he told Felix, and then looked at Madison.

She pursed her lips, opened her mouth, and looked for a second like she was going to say something encouraging—then finally told him, "Don't mess this up, Blackwood!"

She and Felix darted out of the shed.

Ethan didn't think he'd ever understand Madison . . . or any girl.

He closed the armor. The wasp hummed to life around him.

He crouched and jumped out of the shed, destroying the roof in the process.

The wasp's wings snapped into place and he shot straight into the air.

• • • 15 • • •

HEROIC CHARGE

ETHAN DID EXACTLY AS FELIX HAD ORDERED—
he flew low. The truth was, as soon as he started flying . . .
he was too scared to do anything else. He dodged and
rolled past tree trunks and rocks and branches, keeping
low and out of sight. If he hit one of those (flying, he
guessed, at two hundred miles an hour), he'd be bug paste.

The acrobatic moves soon became easy, though. It felt
like Ethan and the wasp swam in slow motion underwater,
able to slide and roll and carve through the air with precision.

What wasn't easy were the doubts that caught up
with him.

He tried to focus on his sister, on how much she de-
pended on him . . . even if she didn't know it.

But his thoughts drifted back to his parents.

For the first time in his life, he *wanted* them to be

different—different because they had only four children when everyone else in the neighborhood had eight or nine—different because they'd raised him and Emma to think on their own and not care what anyone else said about them—and different because with all his heart, Ethan hoped that they weren't part of the mind-controlled alien Collective that would make them . . . well, *not* real parents.

He crossed the mountain ridge and zoomed down the barren slope.

He'd be easy to spot, so he quickly ducked into a crevasse. From there he could see the desert wasteland where the Geo-Transit Tunnel emerged.

Nothing had tried to stop him . . . so he figured nothing had seen him.

So far, so good.

Although there were plenty of things out there *to* see him.

At least twenty drones patrolled the airspace along the train tracks. He spotted a few of the smaller red-and-black wasps darting by too. Those worried him. Madison's dragonfly had fought those. They were nimble and fast.

He wondered if his wasp's stealth mode affected other wasps. Was the stealth mode even on? He wished this wasp armor came with an instruction manual.

There was a glint of silver on one view screen by the tunnel entrance.

Ethan squinted. The wasp magnified the image for him.

It was nothing but a mirage ripple.

But then colored filters and strange symbols and targeting circles swarmed over the ghostly form. The monitor turned black and white and Ethan saw the outline of an ant lion. Its silver armor was near-perfect camouflage.

The last thing he wanted to see was one of *those* things again.

He shuddered . . . and got a bad feeling.

"Pull back the view," he told the wasp.

The black-and-white image on-screen zoomed back out.

Ethan gasped.

There were a dozen ant lions clinging to the side of the cliff, clustered around the tunnel. Also, on the ground, set every fifty feet along the train tracks, there was a dimple in the dirt. In the center of each depression were silver camouflaged jaws, black beady eyes staring out, and the snout tip of an artillery cannon. *More ant lions.*

This was bad. Anything that got close to the train tracks or the tunnel would get blasted before it could shoot back. He'd imagined he'd be able to blow up the tracks by lining up a shot—fly down the track's length so he wouldn't miss and would cause maximum damage. The way those ant lions were positioned, though, he'd be lucky to get one flyby shot before they took him out.

"Felix? Madison? Can you hear me?"

There was a burst of static; then Felix answered, "Roger that, Blackwood. We just got to the suits. Stand by."

"Well, stand by is all I *can* do. When you said the train

would be guarded, you weren't kidding! Ant lions are everywhere—around the tunnel, and covering the tracks as far as I can see."

There was a long pause, and then Felix said, "Madison's ETA is sixty seconds. Hang tight."

Ethan nodded. That was a dumb thing to do because no one could see him. "Got it," he said.

Two of his cameras swiveled and focused on the horizon. They showed a magnified image.

A train.

It magnetically levitated over the tracks, a speeding blur that Ethan knew had a top speed (thanks to last Thursday's science class) of 350 miles per hour.

"Train's coming," he said, and heard his voice waver. "It'll be here in a lot less than a minute."

"I'm kicking in my afterburners," Madison said over her radio, and the channel filled with thunder. "Revised ETA thirty seconds." In the distance a sonic boom echoed.

But the train was already halfway to the tunnel. Ethan guessed it'd be there in *ten* seconds.

"It's safe once it's in the tunnel," Ethan whispered.

"Don't panic," Felix said. "If the train goes in, it'll eventually come out. We have time. Don't do anything stupid."

"When it comes back, it'll be full of students . . . and my sister. We can't risk destroying it then."

Ethan pushed off from his hiding place and took to the air.

"Sorry, Felix, I've got to do this, even if it is stupid."

"Ethan, don't!"

He flew as fast as he could.

Ethan had to destroy the train *before* it got to the tunnel—destroy it in such a way that the Ch'zar couldn't just clear the tracks and send another.

The world around him blurred with speed.

The train rocketed toward the tunnel.

He had to time this just right. He'd get one, and only one, shot.

Of course, Ethan knew very well that he'd pay for this one shot.

His wasp wings clicked into place at a minimal angle, laid nearly flat back against the insect body. On either side jet engines popped out and roared with fire and power.

The train was seconds from the tunnel.

Drones banked toward Ethan's wasp and opened fire.

Laser flashes filled the air and burned his side. He twisted into a barrel roll.

Dozens of ant lion turrets aimed at him. There were eruptions from the earth.

Thunder and black clouds blossomed around him.

Shrapnel slashed through the wasp. Half his view screens went dead. Something punctured his leg and sent a wave of white-hot pain through his body.

He kept going.

He was pure blinding speed, pointed at where he thought the train would be in a few seconds.

"Ethan!" Madison cried. "Pull back! I'm here."

He smiled. "Thanks," he whispered to her, "for finally using my first name."

The engine entered the tunnel—the second car—the third, half of it anyway—until Ethan grabbed it.

His wasp latched on with all six hooked limbs, flared its wings, angled its jets up, pulled and strained and flew as hard as it could.

He ripped the train off the tracks and crashed it into the tunnel mouth—then released it and arced up into the sky.

Ethan caught a split-second flash view of the rest of the high-speed bullet train piling into the wreckage, fountaining sparks, ramming derailed cars farther into the tunnel, compacting metal, and then an explosion mushroomed out of the tunnel.

It was a complete and glorious mess!

He'd done it! It would take forever to clean up and clear the tracks and tunnel.

Emma would be safe . . . for a while.

But his happiness lasted only a fraction of a heartbeat— then an artillery shell hit him square in the thorax.

The world detonated into black stars.

∘ ∘ ∘ 16 ∘ ∘ ∘

SEED BANK

ETHAN HADN'T EXPECTED TO WAKE UP . . .
so when he did, he did so with a grin on his face.

He was alive—definitely alive, because when he
shifted, the pain in his leg turned that grin into a grimace.

He'd slept facedown. His pillow was stained with drool
and a little blood. As he struggled to sit upright, he felt his
busted lip and one eye tender and swollen.

Ethan's smile faded as he saw PROPERTY OF NORTHSIDE
ELEMENTARY stenciled on his pillow.

His heart sank.

He was back in Santa Blanca. They'd caught him.

A gentle hand helped him sit up. It belonged to an old
man sitting in the chair next to his cot. The man had
long white hair and a crooked smile, and he wore a white
lab coat.

The room they were in was tiny. There was just space enough for the cot, a sink, a toilet, a locker, and the chair.

"You had quite a bang-up," the old man said. "We weren't sure we'd find anything alive when we popped open the Infiltrator I.C.E."

Unlike when Ethan woke up yesterday with his memories scrambled, today he remembered everything—Coach Norman showing him how the Ch'zar had "saved" the world—the bus ride toward Sterling Reform School—escaping thanks to Felix and Madison—and then their mission to destroy the train.

Which he'd done . . . and now had to pay the price for it.

No matter what they did to him next, Ethan had won some small victory.

There were some questions he wanted answered, though.

First, he was curious about the old man. He was older than anyone Ethan had ever seen. His skin had wrinkles on its wrinkles. He creaked when he moved. But his eyes glittered with the same wild intensity that shone in Madison's eyes.

Ethan hadn't seen anyone like him in Santa Blanca. He'd been told that when people got this old, they retired to some resort in the tropics.

That had to be a lie, of course. What did the Ch'zar do with old people?

The second thing on Ethan's mind was his leg.

It hurt. He was in shorts, and the exposed bruised and scraped thigh had a large yellow-spotted bandage wrapped around it.

He poked at it.

The bandage squirmed!

Ethan jumped and yelped.

"Don't fiddle with that," the old man told him. "It's alive, but it's perfectly safe. A bit of technology we picked up from our 'friends.' Presently it's repairing a nick on your femoral artery . . . and keeping you alive."

Ethan withdrew his hand.

Was it a caterpillar? A slug? Ick! He tried not to gag.

"You're probably wondering what happened after the train." The old man eased back into his chair. "Let me begin by introducing myself. I am Dr. Gordon Irving, chief scientist and head curmudgeon of this facility."

Ethan didn't know what he meant by "this facility," but he did know what a curmudgeon was. He'd studied that word for last month's spelling bee: C-U-R-M-U-D-G-E-O-N.

It meant a grouch, but that didn't seem to fit the half smile on the old man's face.

"If you expect me to tell you things," Ethan said, gathering his courage, "I can save you the trouble. I'm not going to tell you mind-controlled slaves anything."

Dr. Irving chuckled. "Good. Very good. But relax, young man. You're not in Santa Blanca."

Ethan picked up the pillow with the PROPERTY OF NORTHSIDE ELEMENTARY stenciled on one side and presented it to Dr. Irving.

"Oh, that. We occasionally 'liberate' supplies from the neighborhoods."

"So . . . where am I?" Ethan asked, perplexed. "What happened?"

"You wrecked the train and lost consciousness," Dr. Irving told him. His smile was gone. "You almost died. The Infiltrator suit switched to autopilot and flew back to base with help from the rest of your team."

Ethan remembered. Felix had programmed his suit to escape—and if it couldn't, to self-destruct.

He gulped and sat up straight. "Felix? Madison? They're okay?"

Dr. Irving pulled a notepad from his lab coat and turned it on. A holographic view screen popped into the air. "Are you two still there? Our new friend is up and ready to say hello."

Madison's and Felix's faces crowded on the monitor.

"Ethan!" Felix said, relieved. "They said you lost a lot of blood."

"They said severe brain damage," Madison added sarcastically. "It's the only way we can explain the numskull stunt you pulled!"

"Mr. Blackwood doesn't need to hear that," Dr. Irving told her. "He has to debrief the colonel as soon as he can walk."

"Of course," Felix said, and immediately looked serious. "Ethan, we'll catch up later. You're in good hands."

Behind him, Madison made a looping "you're crazy" gesture at her head.

Dr. Irving turned off the display and slipped it back into his lab coat. "Can you stand? Colonel Winter doesn't like to be kept waiting."

There was a chill in the doctor's tone that made Ethan believe you didn't keep this colonel waiting . . . not unless you wanted serious trouble.

Ethan tested his leg. It ached, but in a good way, like he'd worked out hard and needed to stretch. "I can walk."

"That's the spirit. While we're walking, I'll show you around, and I'll answer any questions you have . . . which I surmise are numerous."

Ethan didn't trust Dr. Irving, but he didn't feel immediately threatened, either. Considering everything that'd happened in the last two days, that was a huge step in the right direction.

"Thanks," Ethan said. "Answers have been in short supply."

"Such is the nature of the universe." Dr. Irving got up and opened the door.

Ethan limped outside.

He and the doctor stood on a long catwalk, a row of steel doors on one side, a railing on the other. A hundred feet below rolled a landscape of farms and irrigating streams, apple orchards and vineyards. It stretched as far as

Ethan could see, but it was strange because there were walls as if this land was a room, a huge room.

Ethan gazed up and saw a ceiling far overhead, crisscrossed with lighted globes so bright, he had to squint to look at them.

"We grow our food here," Dr. Irving explained. "It's part of our heritage."

Far below, people tended the fields, rode electric tractors, herded sheep and cattle—even ostriches and ibex and zebra, species that Ethan thought were supposed to be extinct.

How could this place exist?

"This way," Dr. Irving said, and guided him by the crook of his elbow down the catwalk.

Ethan limped along.

"Felix told you of the Resistance? How when the Ch'zar came, a few people underground were able to resist their mind control?" Dr. Irving made a grand gesture. "*This* is that underground place."

"I don't get it," Ethan said. "If you made this place, or if it was some government base, wouldn't a bunch of people on the surface know about it? And then the Ch'zar would've taken them over and known about it too. Why haven't they come here? Or bombed you from orbit?"

"Indeed . . ." Dr. Irving escorted Ethan onto a circular staircase.

They climbed up the stairs hewn through the solid rock.

"If anyone on the surface *had* known where we were," Dr. Irving said, "we would have been destroyed."

He paused on the stairs to catch his breath. "You know that long ago there was a war among people, all nations fighting one another, half the Earth in flames?"

"Some adults in Santa Blanca told me about it when they tried to get me to talk. It was true?"

"Yes. I was there."

The staircase ended, and they walked down a hall as big as the Geo-Transit Tunnel. On either side were metal doughnuts the size of houses. Electrical arcs and sparks danced on their spiky condensers.

"We darn near blew the world into radioactive bits," Dr. Irving said. "But then some very rich people decided to preserve what was left. This place was built to be a Seed Bank—a haven where plants and animals were to be kept safe. When the war was over, the Seed Bank was to provide the means to renew the Earth. Perhaps it will yet."

Dr. Irving waved at the enormous energy reactors. "The founders provided power, water, and food to last for a hundred years. They also provided for men and women to take care of the Seed Bank."

"So these caretakers were underground when the Ch'zar came?"

"Yes," Dr. Irving replied, "but more important, no one involved in the Seed Bank project—even its rich founders on the surface—knew the location. That was the point. If anyone on the outside knew, some enemy government might destroy us."

"So the Ch'zar couldn't read anyone's mind to find you."

"Precisely. When the Earth was invaded, it took us weeks to piece together what had happened . . . and figure out that the adults here could never go outside. Only our children." Dr. Irving sighed, then looked at Ethan. His face brightened. "Come, you'll enjoy this."

They emerged in a huge chamber that could have been an aircraft hangar. Purple light flooded the room from tubes on the walls. Instead of planes or helicopters, though, the hangar had I.C.E. fighting suits, hundreds of them—beetles and dragonflies, moths with silk wings the size of hang gliders, dog-sized aphids . . . and wasps.

Technicians in white coveralls clustered around the suits. They attached computer monitors and adjusted exoskeleton parts with power air tools. Radiation and biohazard warning stickers were everywhere.

Ethan knew which suit he'd used—its exoskeleton chipped, one antenna broken, and one slender diamond-membrane wing ripped. It had living bandages plastered all over it just like the one on Ethan's leg.

There was a fist-sized hole in its thorax. Shrapnel must have punctured the suit and Ethan's leg, and if it'd been a little higher . . . he would've been killed.

Ethan felt a pang in his chest as if he'd been hit in the same spot. He took a step toward the suit.

The wasp's one remaining antenna lifted toward him.

"Better not, young man," Dr. Irving whispered. "You apparently have a strong bond with that Infiltrator suit . . . an unusually strong one. We need to study it a bit before you fly again. When it comes to human-insect telepathic connections, we've learned to be cautious."

Ethan *had* made a connection. It'd been easy to sink into the wasp's mind. Ethan had felt safe . . . part of something larger than himself. It would've been very easy to stay inside that thing's head.

He shuddered and shook off the feeling.

"Yeah, maybe you're right about that," he whispered. "How many I.C.E. suits do you have?"

"Hundreds," Dr. Irving said. "With thousands more in the incubation bins. We're always finding new species and experimenting on enhancing their capabilities."

Ethan wanted to see them all. Sure, they were gross and weird, but powerful, too . . . and he had to admit he could get very used flying them.

"We always need good pilots," Dr. Irving said, and his crooked smile returned. He nodded at a set of elevator doors across the hangar. "We'll take a closer look another time."

"Yes," Ethan said. "Please."

He spared one last glance at the broken wasp—*his* broken wasp.

It felt wrong to leave it behind, but he let Dr. Irving escort him into the elevator.

Dr. Irving pushed a button. There must have been at least fifty other buttons in the elevator . . . fifty more levels to this place? It had to be huge.

The elevator doors shut, and they were whisked deeper into the earth.

"How long have you been here?" Ethan asked.

"Since the start," Dr. Irving replied. "I was one of those rich men who decided to do something better with his money than buy stocks. One who thought the Seed Bank too important to leave in the care of anyone else."

"And you haven't been outside since . . . ?"

"Not in over fifty years." He sighed. "If I ever stepped outside, the Ch'zar would have my mind and learn everything I know. All the good we've done here would be lost."

Ethan was quiet the rest of the elevator ride.

Dr. Irving had lived most of his life down here. Had he had children? And had they fought the Ch'zar? They must have gotten old and had to stop before they hit puberty. Maybe they'd had kids as well, like Felix and Madison— three generations of Resistance fighters living underground.

Funny how it was the last humans who had to burrow under the earth . . . and how the insects now ruled the world above.

Ethan felt a little claustrophobic.

The elevator halted and the doors opened.

They walked down a narrow concrete tunnel. Water dripped from the ceiling. There was a thick steel door at the end of the tunnel.

Dr. Irving went to knock on it, but the door clicked and opened before he did.

A middle-aged woman stood before them, hands on her hips. Her dark hair was streaked white down the center. She wore a blue military uniform and had a pistol strapped to her hip.

She looked down at Ethan. "Mr. Blackwood," she said. "I don't know if I should kiss you—or march you in front of a firing squad and have you shot!"

° ° ° 17 ° ° °

THE CH'ZAR'S NEW PLAN

COLONEL WINTER'S OFFICE HAD A MAHOGANY desk and bookshelves that crowded two of the walls. Ethan spotted the complete works of Shakespeare, army special operations manuals, and several well-worn volumes of something called *Foxfire* on those shelves.

There was a snow globe of Mount Fuji on her desk.

The colonel sat in a leather executive chair and examined Ethan, then Dr. Irving, before her gaze settled back on Ethan.

There were no chairs for visitors in her office, so they had to stand.

Ethan couldn't stare too long into her steely eyes. Instead, he looked behind her.

On one wall hung pictures of Madison and Felix and a dozen other kids. Some stood in front of I.C.E. suits, some saluted adults, some had broken arms and missing teeth, some were happy, others devastated with sorrow . . . but all of the kids looked strong and proud.

Most of the photos were of Felix.

Ethan gathered his nerve and looked back at Colonel Winter. She and Felix had the same flat nose, diamond-hard glare, and broad shoulders.

He would've bet a year's allowance she and Felix were related.

Ethan swallowed the lump in his throat. He didn't have an allowance anymore. He didn't have a home . . . or parents, either. Now wasn't the time to think of them.

But he couldn't stop.

Ethan blinked away the tears welling in his eyes. He wouldn't cry in front of Dr. Irving and the colonel like some little baby.

"Mr. Blackwood." Colonel Winter closed the manila folder in front of her. It was the one Madison had stolen—Ethan's school record. "You're a fighter," she said. "Your school counselor reports that other kids teased you, but you didn't knuckle under. You fought back, won them over, and became the captain of their soccer team. You are a leader, too."

Ethan shook his head. "It doesn't matter. None of that was real."

"It *was* real," Dr. Irving said. "The Ch'zar very much wanted it to be real. They want the additions to their Collective to be the best and brightest . . . and that would have been you, young man."

Ethan felt dizzy and wished there was a chair.

"Are you *still* a fighter, Mr. Blackwood?" the colonel asked.

"Ma'am?"

She took down a picture of Felix when he was a little kid and looked at it. "I'm asking what you want to do." The chiseled features of her face softened. "I can't imagine what it feels like—to learn that everything you know— your mother and father—that *every* adult wasn't what they seemed to be." She shook her head, and the strength returned to her features. "But you have a decision to make. You can stay here underground with us, safe, and never have to face the Ch'zar again."

She set the picture of Felix aside. "Or you can join the battle. I've seen the initial reports of your remarkable skills in the Infiltrator I.C.E. We can put you to good use."

Ethan enjoyed flying, but the lasers and bombs and battling for his life . . . he wasn't sure if he could do that again.

"I don't know," Ethan whispered.

"Really, Barbara," Dr. Irving said. "Is it necessary that we do this *now* with him?"

"Mr. Blackwood needs to hear this, and the rest of the truth. He has talent, but he needs training before he hurts himself or his teammates." The colonel looked him up and down with disapproval. "And most of all, he needs *discipline.*"

Dr. Irving tossed up his hands in a gesture of surrender.

"Because," Colonel Winter said, her tone darkening, "if you were under my command and went off on your own—I don't care if you took out a legion of ant lion mobile artillery or a squadron of enemy interceptor wasps. I would've pinned a medal on your chest, and kept you under house arrest for the rest of your life!"

Ethan flinched. He was pretty sure she meant it.

Hadn't she mentioned something about a firing squad, too? His gaze lingered on the pistol holstered on her hip. It had a carved ivory handle inlaid with silver stars.

"But I won," he whispered. "I stopped that train."

"So you did," the colonel said, "but you did so with reckless abandon for your life, and placed your team in danger. The I.C.E. suits are designed to work *together*. One suit's strength protects your teammates' weaknesses. Working together is the only way to survive out there."

She touched a button on her desk.

The wood pattern was replaced with a three-dimensional map, showing deserts and mountains and a serene valley. It was night, and stars sparkled overhead like a river of diamond dust.

Colonel Winter tapped another button, and the view took on a green glow. Now Ethan could see the contour lines of mountains, and clouds blowing by with tiny arrows indicating direction and speed.

"That's Santa Blanca," he said.

"Specifically, the Appalachian Sector of the Ch'zar's

neighborhood network," Dr. Irving told him. "There are six communities in the region."

The map zoomed in on the Geo-Transit Tunnel. Both train tracks and highway were ruined. It looked real. Tiny ant lions cleared rubble from the tunnel mouth. As soon as they cleared one boulder, three more crumbled and fell off the slope overhead.

Dr. Irving snorted and smiled at this. "And, indeed, you've temporarily saved the children there from their respective fates. This places the Ch'zar in a bind. They have to get those older children out before they're absorbed and the younger children notice."

"That's good, right?" Ethan asked. "We can go back and rescue them before they change!"

Emma was one of those kids . . . about to become part of the Ch'zar Collective.

Colonel Winter and Dr. Irving shared a quick look, the same one Felix and Madison had used to silently communicate with each other.

Dr. Irving's smile vanished. "The Ch'zar have made up their minds to get the children out."

Felix had told Ethan that once the aliens made up their minds, it was almost impossible for them to change.

"They're not waiting to clear your well-demolished tunnel," Colonel Winter said. She waved her hand. The display pulled back a mile over the landscape. A pair of silver clouds sat motionless in the air.

"We hacked into one of the enemy satellites," she explained. "This is a live feed."

The colonel stabbed at the two silver objects. They magnified and refocused.

They were tapering cylinders, engines mounted along their sides, and underneath hung a cabin that looked like it could hold a hundred passengers.

"Zeppelins?" Ethan asked. "That's antique technology."

"The Ch'zar re-created these from Earth's historical records," Dr. Irving said. "Why they aren't using airplanes or helicopters is a mystery to us as well."

Ethan reached toward the image and stretched his hands like the colonel had. The display's view returned to high over the valley. He looked at the tiny houses nestled there.

His blood ran cold.

They were coming for Emma and the other students about to go off to high school.

"When?" he asked.

"Dawn," Colonel Winter told him. "There's more."

In quick succession she highlighted sectors of airspace. Glowing dots appeared. "Seven Mirage-class dragonflies escort the zeppelins. Interceptor wasps and surveillance drones patrol the entire valley."

She touched the outskirts of town, and six blobs lit blue. "A legion of bombardier beetles there."

The colonel tapped Emerald Park next to Northside

Elementary. "The zeppelins will likely land here, as the four acres of grass have been mined with ant lion artillery. Rhinoceros beetles are scattered throughout the foothills. Squads of fast-strike Thunderbolt-class locusts are hidden in farmlands to blanket Santa Blanca with offensive capability."

Ethan took it all in.

It was horrifying, but he understood their strategy. There was a goal, defenders, and strikers—like in a soccer match.

He wished he knew how fast his wasp could fly. How hard was it to detect in stealth mode? How tough were those Thunderbolt-class locusts?

He needed help from Felix and Madison.

Better yet . . . there were *hundreds* of fighting suits in the hangar.

A plan took shape in his head.

Ethan ran through it, speaking out loud. "We'll use dragonfly Reconnaissance I.C.E.s to scout the enemies' positions. They can draw fire, if necessary, and then get away quick. Rhinoceros beetles will engage the locusts at the edge of town. Meanwhile, a squadron of our wasps flies in and takes out the real targets. The zeppelins."

He looked up from the map. "How many pilots do you have?"

The colonel's lips pressed into a thin white line. "We have twenty-seven on the active-duty roster. Your plan *might* work only if you had twice that many."

"But we have a chance to save those people." Ethan's face flushed. "Isn't that worth any risk?"

"*Any* risk . . . ?" The colonel's face flushed too. "No."

Dr. Irving cleared his throat and said, "Let me, Barbara." He turned to Ethan. "Your plan is tactically sound and your bravery is admirable, young man. I know you'd risk your life to save your sister."

Ethan crossed his arms.

Of course they knew about Emma. They had his school file.

They probably thought that was all Ethan cared about, but they were missing the bigger picture.

"This isn't just about my sister," he said. "There are half a dozen other kids who'll be taken. Five more neighborhoods— thirty lives at stake!"

"But so are the lives of our pilots," Dr. Irving told him.

Ethan frowned. "I'll admit there's some risk. We could win, though."

Dr. Irving held up one finger. "I do not deny the possibility. But what if you lost even one pilot? The Ch'zar would dissect that I.C.E. suit and learn our secrets. What if the unthinkable happened . . . and you lost *all* our pilots?"

Ethan hadn't thought about losing. That wasn't how you went into a match. You focused on winning.

But this wasn't a game of soccer with points and penalty flags. People might get hurt. Maybe killed.

He suddenly wasn't so sure.

The colonel waved at the three-dimensional map, and her desk returned to normal.

"I know how you feel, Mr. Blackwood," she whispered. "Every day we lose many more than thirty neighborhood children to the enemy. And every day I feel it. This is not just one battle, though. We fight for all of humanity."

Ethan took a step back.

He took a deep breath.

He couldn't let the Ch'zar take Emma.

But he wouldn't risk *everything* and *everyone* here at the Seed Bank, either.

"I get it," he whispered, and hung his head.

Ethan had never felt so helpless. So small.

A REBEL AMONG REBELS

ETHAN SAT ON THE COT IN HIS NEW ROOM feeling sorry for himself.

He stuffed those bad feelings deep inside and tried instead to come up with a way to save his sister.

He couldn't risk the lives of the pilots in the Resistance to save her. And even if he *was* willing to do that . . . Colonel Winter wouldn't let him.

Once those kids from Santa Blanca got on the zeppelins, how would Ethan be able to attack the aircraft without hurting the very people he was trying to save?

Dawn was just a few hours away. Time was running out.

And why use zeppelins? Why not a jet or a helicopter? The Ch'zar could have been in Santa Blanca by now. Why be slow *on purpose*?

Ethan looked at his bruised and scraped hands. Two

days ago everything had been going his way, and the entire world had made sense.

Now . . . nothing did.

There was a tap at his door.

"Come in," Ethan said, although visitors were the last thing he wanted.

Felix opened the steel door. He looked almost normal in jeans and a black T-shirt.

"You okay, Ethan?"

"I just need time to think," Ethan said.

Felix's forehead wrinkled with concern. "I understand. We'll talk tomorrow. Take all the time you need, buddy."

That was the problem. There was no time left.

Madison pushed the big guy aside and moved into Ethan's room. She wore green sweats. Her hair was wet. She was no longer a blonde—rather, her hair was jet-black.

"I've got something to tell you," she said, and flashed a defiant look at Felix.

"Why don't you give the guy a break, Mad?" He looked sympathetically at Ethan.

"Let her say whatever she wants," Ethan said.

Ethan figured he had it coming. She and Felix had probably rushed in and risked their lives to save his neck after he wrecked the train and the wasp.

Madison stomped a foot at Felix. "Just leave, would you?"

She gritted her teeth and wrung her hands as if it was uncomfortable for her to be in the same room as Ethan.

Felix eased out of the room. "Shout if you need me," he said to Ethan. "I'll bring help." He clicked the door shut.

Ethan guessed Madison wanted some privacy to slug him in the face. Instead, she surprised him and sat on the cot—as far away from Ethan as possible. She looked at the floor.

"Going off on your own to take out that train," she said, "was the most moronic thing anyone's ever done in the history of the universe."

"I didn't have a choice."

She sat in silence for a long time, and finally she told him, "I get it."

Understanding was the last thing Ethan expected from her.

"I know how you feel," she said.

Ethan didn't want her sympathy. She hadn't been raised by parents who'd turned out to be something else. She didn't have sisters or a brother who would one day be slaves to some alien empire.

"How could you know anything about what I'm feeling?"

"I do," she whispered. Her head dropped and her hair fell over her face so Ethan couldn't see her expression. "My brother . . ." Her voice choked off.

Ethan's thoughts about his own misery and family screeched to a halt.

He'd been so stupid. He should've guessed this before.

"Your brother was the third member of your team? The pilot of the wasp?"

She nodded and wiped her eyes. "Roger was a year older than me," she said. "He *had* to save those kids. It was the first solid lead we had—we knew where and when they'd be taken by the Ch'zar. But he had this thing on his neck covered with a Band-Aid. He told me it was a nick he'd gotten working the hydraulics on his suit. I should have known it was a *pimple*. We're all trained to watch for them. It's one of the first signs of puberty. And I should've known he'd be stubborn and arrogant enough to think he could do one last mission."

She ran a hand over her neck, smoothing the skin, unthinkingly feeling for any blemish.

"An hour out from Santa Blanca, Roger had trouble flying," Madison said. "The radio malfunctioned and he landed. At first, Felix and I thought it was the suit. That particular wasp I.C.E. is tricky to work. It's always trying to dominate its pilots. In fact, Dr. Irving thought for a long time that we'd have to destroy it. Roger was one of the few to ever control the thing. He said it was the best wasp he'd ever flown."

"So it landed," Ethan said, leaning closer. "What happened then?"

"It turns out Roger *was* having trouble with the wasp, but not like we thought. It'd been sensing the change in him . . . I guess it could feel him getting absorbed into the

Collective." She took a deep breath. "And so the wasp grounded and ejected him. Roger tried to get back inside, but the cockpit sealed and locked. That's when the Band-Aid on his neck fell off and I saw that pimple—that's when the wasp poised in an aggressive threat stance—and that's when Felix and I knew for sure what'd happened to him."

Madison laced her hands in her lap and huddled inward.

"Roger said we should come with him, that the Ch'zar's way was best. If we could see what he was seeing, for even an instant, then we'd understand."

Madison let out a shuddering sigh. "One second he'd been my brother . . . then he wasn't. Felix rushed him. Roger used one of our own flash-bang grenades on us, and he got away."

Ethan wanted to put a hand on her shoulder to comfort her.

He decided not to. Sure, it would have been the same consoling gesture he'd used before with his soccer teammates after they'd lost a match . . . but it'd also feel a little like when he'd held Mary Vincent's hand at the Sadie Hawkins dance.

That would've felt just too weird between Madison and him.

"Why didn't you set the wasp's self-destruct?" Ethan asked. "Roger—the Ch'zar—they would have known where it'd grounded and come for it."

Madison nodded. "Yeah, that's what I said, too. But Felix decided that any I.C.E. suit that could detect and fight a pilot under Ch'zar influence was worth trying to save. If Dr. Irving could figure out what made the wasp so smart, maybe every I.C.E. could be bred that way. So we half dragged and half flew the suit a mile up the mountain to that cave. Felix had found the place on another mission, one without Roger, so it'd be hard for the Ch'zar to locate. Then we had to find a pilot stubborn enough for the wasp to accept—at least enough so its autopilot would kick in."

"Me," Ethan said.

"You," she replied.

She set a leather wristband between them on the cot. Laced on it was a bead with red, blue, white, and gold stripes.

"He took this off before he left," she told Ethan. "It's an electrical resistor. Roger's idea. He gave each of us one. We're Resisters—spelled with an *e*. This is a resistor—with an *o*. Get it? Ha-ha."

Ethan had seen electrical resistors when they'd studied circuits in science class.

"It's cool," he said.

"He was telling us we need symbols and heroes to take risks to inspire everyone." She looked up. Tears streaked her cheeks. "Like you did for your sister." She nodded at the wristband. "Keep it."

"I . . . I couldn't," Ethan said. "It was your brother's."

"You earned it." She got up and went to the door. "*You* destroyed that train, and that's what Roger wanted more than anything . . . to finish that stupid mission."

Madison swung open the door with a violent motion.

She paused and said, "It's lights-out in five minutes. They take that seriously around here. Guards patrol every ten minutes. So stay in your room, Blackwood."

She was back to calling him Blackwood and not Ethan anymore. Great.

"I should have done more to save my brother," Madison whispered. She looked away, and said so softly that he barely heard, "You better do whatever it takes to save the people you love . . . or you'll regret it for the rest of your life."

She left and gently shut the door.

Ethan couldn't believe it. Was she saying that he should go save his sister? After she'd chewed him out for trying to save her the first time?

What about risking everyone else's lives? Or keeping the Resisters a secret?

Why were girls *always* so confusing?

He picked up the wristband. The electrical resistor was scuffed. It'd seen a lot of action. It was something someone a lot tougher than him would wear.

A fighter would wear this. A rebel. A Resister.

He set it down. It wasn't his.

The lights in his room went out.

A line of illumination filtered in from under the door.

Now what? Sit here in the dark and keep thinking? Eventually fall asleep? And when he woke up, Ethan would've lost his sister.

What else could he do?

Madison had said: *You better do whatever it takes to save the people you love . . . or you'll regret it for the rest of your life.*

Coach Norman had told Ethan: *Superior long-range strategy always wins over superior immediate tactics.*

And suddenly Ethan knew what he had to do.

He had run away from his first fight with the Ch'zar. He wasn't ashamed that he'd been scared on the mountaintop. Anyone would have . . . the first time.

The second time he'd run away, he'd left Felix and Madison behind in a desperate attempt to save Emma . . . and ended up putting their lives at risk in the process.

And now?

Yes, he was scared. Scared to death. But he *was* going to fight.

And yes, he was desperate, but he had a strategy this time. He wouldn't be risking anyone's life but his own.

Muffled voices came from the catwalk outside.

Two shadows flashed under the door.

Those had to be the patrolling guards.

According to Madison, they patrolled every ten minutes . . . so he'd have to move fast.

As soon as he could no longer hear them, Ethan eased the door open—and he ran.

∘ ∘ ∘ 19 ∘ ∘ ∘

GOING HOME

ETHAN HALF CREPT, HALF JOGGED DOWN the catwalk.

It was nighttime in the huge farmland cavern. Crickets chirped. The lights on the ceiling were dim and looked like moons in the sky.

He spiraled up the stairs to the hallway of fusion reactors. Their sparking glow lit his way.

Ethan kept to the shadows. A pair of adult guards tromped up the stairs behind him, and Ethan ducked behind one of the house-sized reactors as they approached.

Static electricity from the reactor made Ethan's hair stand straight up.

They passed . . . and didn't see him.

He exhaled the breath he'd been holding, waited a minute, and then continued toward the hangar.

Ethan passed several doorways he hadn't noticed earlier. He peered inside and saw caverns glowing with bioluminescent blues and greens and filled with thousands and thousands of insect eggs, some as large and colorful as beach balls, others the size of baseballs that looked like solid gold, and still others as big as cars, bumpy and black.

There were also bulbous pupa cases with pulsing and squirming things inside.

Gross . . . and so cool. What other kinds of bugs did they have? Ones that flew, burrowed, or swam? What kinds of modifications had they made to them?

But his curiosity had to wait.

If he survived one more day, he'd let someone else do all the hero stuff. Ethan would ask Dr. Irving if he could become his assistant. Then he could learn all he wanted—in a safe laboratory.

He tiptoed into the hangar.

Hundreds of giant insects stood motionless, hooked up to electronic monitors and beeping computers. Occasionally an insect leg would twitch, as if the bugs dreamed.

They were supercreepy.

He saw a dozen wasps, but none of them was the wasp Ethan knew he could fly.

Had it been taken away? Had it died?

He felt a cold lump in his chest.

Something told him it wasn't dead, though.

Ethan turned and moved toward the back of the

hangar. It was so dark there he could barely see . . . but he could feel a familiar presence.

His eyes adjusted, and he saw the outline of a wasp. As his eyes adjusted more, he saw those weird caterpillar bandages plastered over its armor. The large hole in its thorax had been welded together. It still only had one antenna, which tracked Ethan as he approached.

"Remember me?" Ethan whispered.

There was a gentle pull at his mind . . . and an invitation to link again with the bug.

Ethan resisted.

He thought it'd be a good idea to heed Dr. Irving's warning: *When it comes to human-insect telepathic connections, we've learned to be cautious.*

"I've got to ask you something."

Ethan hadn't planned this part. What he'd planned was to risk his own life—fly off alone to Santa Blanca, grab Emma, and fly out before anything could stop him.

He'd forgotten that he'd be risking the wasp's life as well.

Okay, it was stupid to ask. Ethan should just get inside the thing and go.

It was alive, though. It was smart, too . . . maybe smarter than any bug here, if Felix was right about it. If it was going to risk its life, then it deserved a vote.

"I need your help," he said. "I want to fly back home. Can you get me there?"

The wasp remained still, the connection in Ethan's mind silent.

He tried again, this time putting more feeling in his thoughts: how much he cared for his sister, and how he needed to protect her.

"We have to save Emma. Maybe grab the twins, too. Their lives are depending on us."

The twins! Ethan had almost forgotten about them. They weren't in imminent danger, but they would be years from now when they grew up.

The wasp didn't respond to his pleas.

Maybe it couldn't fly anymore. Maybe it was too injured. Maybe this whole plan wouldn't work.

Ethan ran through it again: get the wasp into stealth mode, fly back low to the ground, and avoid all contact.

What if those rhinoceros beetles or locusts got in his way?

He'd blast them quick! Use the wasp's lasers to disable them and slow them down. Hadn't Madison said the Infiltrator model was designed to be best at running combat?

His blood raced at the thought of combat—flying, dodging, blasting, and ripping things.

Ethan was part terrified, part pulse-thumpingly excited.

The connection between him and the wasp strengthened.

It was thinking of fighting too. It *wanted* to fight.

The armor on the wasp's cockpit slid aside. The interior lights winked on, welcoming him.

Ethan gulped. Sure, they might need to fight . . . but he'd engage the enemy only as a last option.

He kept that thought to himself, however, as he climbed into the I.C.E. suit.

The tiny breathing holes on the wall blasted cool air on him, and the cockpit closed. View screens lit, and status indicators rainbowed to life around him.

Ethan hardly noticed the fluid as it filled the suit's limbs. The gel probably cushioned the jostling from sudden acceleration and combat.

There was one thing to take care of before he left, though.

Ethan licked his lips, took a deep breath, and tapped the same controls he'd seen Felix touch to set the suit to self-destruct. If the suit got too damaged or fell into the power of the Ch'zar, it'd blow itself up.

The wasp had no reaction to this, so it must've been okay with it too.

Ethan wished he understood a fraction of the controls before him. He didn't like having to rely on the wasp.

"Let's fly out of here," Ethan said. "Take me to Santa Blanca. Go fast—but save some fuel for a quick getaway, in case we need one."

The wasp pulled free of rigging lines and electrical hookups. It landed on the hangar floor with a thud.

Its carapace split, and wings unfolded and ruffled. They seemed stiff.

Maybe the beast needed to recover from its injuries. Maybe it couldn't fly at all.

The wings beat faster, and the air resonated with their

buzz. Then they moved so fast, they blurred to near invisible.

The wasp's jets sparked and roared to life—and they took off!

They zoomed through the dark to the far end of the hangar.

Ethan was positive they were going to fly straight into the wall, but at the last moment the wasp veered straight up, twisting Ethan's stomach into a pretzel.

A tunnel wormed through the ceiling into the solid rock.

They twisted and dodged and kept climbing. Every twenty feet, tiny winking lights illuminated a patch of the perilous passage. Jagged rocks loomed from the walls. They looked like teeth that could slice the suit in half if they crashed.

Faint moonlight lit the rock walls. They were almost out!

Every view screen then went black.

"Hey!"

Ethan tapped the central monitor. "Turn these things back on."

Had the wasp malfunctioned?

He tried to force the wasp's eyes to open, but the connection between him and the insect was blank.

The words *SECURITY PROTOCOL 003* flashed across Ethan's mind and remained there a moment, like a blurry afterimage left by a bright light.

What did that mean? "Security" for what?

Of course! Security to protect the biggest secret the Resisters had: *their location.*

Ethan guessed that pilots had to fly out blind on auto-pilot.

Once outside, he'd bet, the autopilot zigged and zagged them on some random course until they were far away—and only then could they look where they were going. Because if Resistance pilots knew where their base was and they ever got captured, it'd be just a matter of time before the Ch'zar would get the pilots' memories and know the location of the base too.

It was a smart setup.

Acceleration slammed Ethan into the contoured support. Then he bounced from side to side as the wasp changed course.

The monitors popped on. Stars and the black outlines of mountains surrounded him. Green night-vision filters overlaid the screens. Targeting circles appeared, tracking deer and bears and even a bat fluttering far off.

Ethan was flying!

He imagined he felt the air rush over his body. He leaned forward and poured on the speed, skimming the treetops.

It was the best feeling in the world.

Then he remembered what he was doing . . . and his excitement died.

Hide, Ethan thought. *Use that 'stealth mode' thing.*

Purple status lights illuminated. The hum of the wasp's wings and jets became a whisper rumble.

One screen popped on showing a map with roads and bridges. There were also lines and shaded zones that grew and shrank as Ethan watched.

The wasp steered clear of those spaces.

Felix and Colonel Winter had talked about the Ch'zar satellite web. Those must be the areas the aliens could see from space.

Ethan and the wasp soared over a mountaintop and then down the other side into wasteland.

There were towering robots that chewed through canyons, countless rolling factories, and millions of mechanical creatures tearing apart the earth.

It made Ethan sad to see them destroying his world . . . and he felt powerless to stop them.

They flew like this for hours, and then the lands greened and sloped up, and the wasp glided over a forested mountainside and over its peaks.

In the distant valley were the winking lights of his neighborhood.

Instead of feeling relief, Ethan dreaded coming back. There were new dangers all around him.

And if he got past the beetles, locusts, drones, and ant lions? More danger. Adults would be everywhere—each a part of the Ch'zar Collective intelligence. If a single one of them spotted him . . . they'd *all* know. They could swarm over him and grab him before he could blink.

Be careful, he urged the wasp.

Reluctance pushed back from the insect's mind . . . but after a split-second hesitation, it throttled back its engines and wings and became *completely* silent.

Ethan held his breath, waiting to get blasted out of the air.

They glided over the roofs of the school, the buildings of Main Street, and houses.

He made it all the way to his house.

Ethan landed better this time, setting down in his backyard, maneuvering the wasp under the large maple tree, and scattering a pile of raked leaves.

The cockpit opened and Ethan clambered out.

In the shadows, the wasp's black-and-gold pattern was excellent camouflage.

He listened. No doors opened. There were no sirens. No cries of alarm.

Good.

Now the hard part. Ethan had to find Emma and explain all this to her . . . without alerting any adults.

But what about his mom and dad? Ethan desperately wanted to believe they were different. He couldn't afford to believe that, though. He had to save Emma and the twins first—then he could risk finding out more about his parents.

He crept up the back porch and into the kitchen.

His stomach rumbled. By habit, Ethan opened the refrigerator door and looked for something to eat.

What was he *doing*? He shut the refrigerator and padded upstairs.

The house had a weird, still feeling that he couldn't put his finger on.

He eased into the twins' room. Their bunk beds were empty. It looked like a tornado had passed through the room (which was normal), but this time the dressers had been opened and their clothes were gone.

It was like they'd left . . . or been taken away in a hurry. Ethan didn't like this.

He snuck into Emma's room next.

It was empty too. But *really* empty. The blankets and sheets on her bed had been stripped off. Her stuff had been packed into boxes labeled: VASSAR PREP H.S./BLACK-WOOD, E. K./EARLY HONORS ADM.

He felt numb and stood staring a moment.

Had the zeppelins come early? Had they already taken her?

There was one last place to check . . . his parents' room. Ethan wasn't ready for that, but he couldn't *not* check, either.

He crept toward their room. The door was open, which was wrong, because they always slept with it shut. He peeked around the corner.

The room was as messy as the twins'.

Franklin and Melinda Blackwood weren't there.

Ethan's hand went to his throat. What if his parents *had been* different . . . and because of all the trouble he'd caused, they'd been found out?

There had to be *some* clue here about what happened.

It looked, though, like someone had already searched for clues. Their clothes had been pulled from the dressers and scattered, the hamper had been overturned, and all the contents of their closet had been tossed onto the floor.

Ethan's breath caught in his throat.

There was a door in the back of the closet . . . only visible because it was partially open. Otherwise, it would have blended with the wall perfectly.

Ethan touched that door—metal and heavy to push. Lead?

The tiny room was lined with lead as well, and a single lightbulb hung from the ceiling. There were two combination safes. Both were open and empty.

Ethan was more confused than ever. He had to keep searching. He had to find something.

He went to his room. The covers on his bed were still neatly pulled aside from when he'd gotten up. The white Blanca Dairy parka lay on the floor where he'd dropped it.

One member of the Blackwood family was still here. Mr. Bubbles. Ethan went to feed his pet betta fish.

A folded piece of paper lay under his fish-food container.

Ethan opened it. In his mom's curlicue handwriting, it read:

Ethan,
    We wish we could explain. If you've come back to save Emma and the twins, though, you must know part of the truth.
    And you know why we cannot explain.
    We have the twins. We'll be safe.
    Emma is likely already at the school. They took her to wait for the zeppelin. There's nothing any of us can do for her now.
    The priority is to save yourself. You're more important to humanity than you can know.
    Be safe, darling. Keep your head.
    It is our wish that one day we'll all be reunited under the open sky—then we will explain everything.

All our love,
Mom and Dad

The letter in his hands blurred. Tears fell on the paper. Why? Why couldn't they have told him any of this stuff?

Why—when he needed them the most—had they left Emma and him?

He crumpled the note in frustration, but stopped . . . and smoothed it.

Of course his parents couldn't say anything. If somehow they had found a way to beat the Ch'zar mind control and were working against the aliens, he and Emma would be the most dangerous people in the world to them.

Emma was on the cusp of becoming an adult, Ethan soon after that . . . and then they'd be absorbed into the Collective.

He folded the note with care and slid it into his pocket.

Ethan hoped that wherever they were, his parents were safe.

Maybe one day, like they said, they'd all be together again.

But until then, there was still time to save Emma.

Ethan tromped downstairs. He had to get back to the wasp, fly to the school—and blast through any guards and obstacles to get inside. He had to get Emma and take her to a safe place, no matter what.

He banged out the back door . . .

. . . and stood face to face with a dozen police, guns leveled at him, and a dozen more adults surrounding them—all staring at him with unblinking eyes, all moving closer.

There was no chance of escape.

LAST CHANCE

ETHAN HAD BEEN DUCT-TAPED TO A METAL folding chair. The chair was in the middle of the school's gym. Bright spotlights shone down on him.

He struggled against the tape—but it was no use. His ankles, knees, elbows, and wrists were bound without any slack.

Ethan shouted and pulled against his bonds anyway. "Let me out of here!"

He couldn't let it end like this.

All he was doing, though, was putting on a show for the adults gathered around him.

Coach Norman was there; the principal; the vice principal; all of Ethan's teachers; Miss Jenkin, the milk lady; even Mary Vincent's and Bobby's parents. Some of them wore suits, but most were in their pajamas. Coach Norman was in his Grizzlies red-and-brown warm-up sweats.

Every one of them watched Ethan. Unblinking.

The two policemen who had taken him in the other day, Officers Grace and Hendrix, stood by the gym's double doors—in robotic athletic suits!

Coach Norman knelt next to him. "Go ahead and struggle, Ethan, but you're *not* getting away this time."

Ethan glared at Coach, but Coach stared back without emotion.

Ethan felt his stomach sink.

Great. Even if he broke free—even if he managed to get past all these mind-controlled adults—he'd have to deal with those hydraulically powered exoskeletons that could swat him out of the way . . . like he was an insect.

"Okay," Ethan said, panting. He bit back all his angry comments. "So what now, Coach?"

Coach ran a hand over his buzz-cut hair. "Now? We get you and the kids aboard the zeppelin and leave." He motioned to Dr. Ray to come over.

Dr. Horatio Ray had given Ethan his inoculations, straightened his sprained finger, and always greeted him with smiling concern. Now, however, Dr. Ray had no expression at all on his face as he handed Coach a hypodermic needle.

"And," Coach said as he took the syringe, "we're going to sedate you. We underestimated you the first time, Ethan . . . *greatly* underestimated you. We don't make the same mistake twice."

Ethan's eyes bulged at the sight of that needle. He squirmed uselessly back into his chair.

"Wait. Wait!" Ethan said. "Just answer a few questions for me. What harm could that do?"

Coach considered. "I don't think so."

He moved the needle closer.

"No!" Ethan's heart raced.

Coach swabbed an ice-cold alcohol patch on Ethan's forearm.

"Wait! We can *trade* information."

Coach hesitated. He stared into the distance, and then he smiled.

"What would you tell us that we're not going to know *after* you join us, Ethan? Are you going to say your Resister friends are on their way to rescue you? There's nothing on our radar or satellite images. You're alone . . . but only for a few more moments."

He touched the needle to Ethan's arm.

"You're wrong," Ethan said. "There's one thing—about the fighting suits."

Coach froze, the needle dimpling Ethan's skin.

Ethan wasn't sure why he'd blurted that out. . . .

Maybe it was because he knew the Ch'zar were interested in those suits. As far as they were concerned, the Ch'zar used humans. This was a case of humans using *their* technology. That had to freak them out.

Plus Felix had said the suits had science the Ch'zar had never developed, like the stealth mode.

There was one more thing.

"There's this bond between the pilot and the suit," Ethan whispered. "Telepathic . . . but not absolute control like you guys use. This is something different. Better."

Coach blinked rapidly. "That's impossible."

The other adults in the auditorium blinked as well and looked back and forth among one another . . . confused.

So they didn't know about it.

Yet they'd captured pilots like Madison's brother. They *had to* know everything the pilots knew.

Ethan bet that whatever connection there was between pilot and suit vanished once a pilot's mind got absorbed into the Ch'zar Collective.

Or maybe even the Resisters didn't fully understand what was going on with the mental link between their pilots and the suits. Dr. Irving had been intrigued (and, it seemed to Ethan, a little scared) by the strength of his connection with his wasp.

"I can tell you more," Ethan said, "but *I* want answers first."

Ethan was playing a dangerous game. There were a few things he had to know, though.

Besides . . . he'd have done anything—*absolutely anything*—to stay awake and alive and Ethan Blackwood a few minutes longer instead of being absorbed.

But he might accidentally give the Ch'zar clues that could destroy the Resisters.

He'd have to be supercareful.

What his parents had written in their note echoed in his thoughts: *You're more important to humanity than you can know. Be safe, darling. Keep your head.*

Coach handed the hypodermic back to Dr. Ray.

"Very well, Ethan," Coach said. "Telling you a few things can't possibly hurt us. And perhaps there is something to what you say."

Coach whispered to the principal and vice principal, who quickly left the auditorium.

"What do you want to know?" Coach asked Ethan.

"My parents. What happened to them?"

"Melinda and Franklin Blackwood were with us . . . but they vanished from our thoughts," Coach said. His gray eyebrows crinkled together. "We were hoping *you* would be able to tell us more. But I can see from your expression you're as much in the dark as we are. Interesting."

Ethan considered this. His mom and dad were "with" them and then "vanished"?

Did Coach mean they were part of the Collective . . . and then *not* part of the Collective?

That didn't make sense. How could someone escape Ch'zar mental domination?

The important thing was the Ch'zar didn't know where his parents were. They'd gotten away!

He wanted to blame his mom and dad for leaving him in this mess, but they'd done the right thing . . . the safe thing . . . the only thing.

There were so many questions. Like why his parents, if

they could escape Ch'zar influence, were raising their children in a neighborhood in the first place?

He set his anger and curiosity aside.

None of that stuff could help him or Emma escape. He needed information about what was happening here and now.

"Why use zeppelins?" Ethan asked. "You could have sent in helicopters to get the kids off to high school in no time."

Coach held up a finger. "My turn to ask a question, son. Tell me about the fighting suit. You control them telepathically?"

"It's *not* control," Ethan said. For some reason Coach's suggesting he "controlled" the wasp like a machine made him mad. "We work *with* them."

This, at least, had been Ethan's experience with the wasp.

Coach shook his head as if he couldn't believe this.

"So about the zeppelins?" Ethan prompted.

Coach nodded. "Those were for *your* benefit, Ethan. And the Resisters'. We knew they'd be watching and planning . . . just like the first time they tried to stop us from taking our children."

Our children.

The way Coach said that . . . like those kids were a snack . . . Ethan shuddered.

"After you surprised us and returned to save your sister," Coach said, "we knew you'd come back again. We had to bait the trap. A jet or helicopter would have re-moved your sister too quickly—before you got here." He shrugged. "Too bad no Resisters came with you."

The police in the exoskeleton athletic suits opened the gym's double doors.

Two large fleas—each the size of a golf cart and cov-ered in wiry copper hairs and jagged red armor—dragged in Ethan's inert wasp.

The I.C.E. fighting suit had curled into a fetal position. It felt sick to Ethan.

The fleas pulled it toward him, scratching and scraping the wasp's barbed limbs across the hardwood gymnasium floor.

They left it at his feet.

"*Show* us this telepathic connection," Coach Norman demanded. "Wake it up. Just a single twitch to prove what you're saying is true."

The fleas took positions on either side of Ethan, sway-ing on their long, hinged legs—ready to strike.

Ethan remembered from biology class that fleas were bloodsuckers and able to jump two hundred times their body length. They were strong enough to rip him to pieces.

The gym doors burst open, and one of the supersized ant lions pushed its way into the gym—demolishing part of the walls to get inside.

It lumbered toward Ethan and stopped a foot away. The artillery gun mounted on its back pointed at the wasp.

Its huge jaws snapped once—twice—inches away from Ethan's face!

If Ethan hadn't been taped to that chair, he would've jumped out of his skin.

"Okay . . . okay!" Ethan screamed. His heart pounded so hard, it felt like it was in his throat. "Whatever you want—just tell these things to back off. I can't concentrate."

Coach Norman nodded.

The ant lion and the fleas scuttled three steps back.

Ethan licked his lips.

He was terrified, but the feeling of panic faded as Ethan stared at the wasp.

He seemed to fall into it . . . or at least his mind fell toward the wasp's . . . until he connected with the insect brain.

It was in a deep sleep, but not like the hibernation mode it'd been in before.

This was different. Wrong.

Ethan concentrated and sensed a hole in the wasp's mind. Something big and important was missing. The self-destruct mechanism?

That made sense. The wasp was supposed to blow itself up if it got into the Ch'zar's control.

They must have gotten it into hibernation mode before it could self-destruct and then somehow erased that part of its programming.

The Ch'zar were already learning some important things about the fighting suit . . . and that was very bad.

He felt the wasp's mind circling around and around that deleted part of its brain, unsure what to do next.

And what was he supposed to do now? Wake the wasp like Coach wanted? Ethan was confident he could, just like the first time he'd roused it from deep hibernation. But would the Ch'zar then use the wasp? Raise hundreds of them to fight the Resisters?

Ethan's thoughts skidded to a halt.

What an idiot! *He* could use it.

Wake the wasp up and let it do what it had been bred to do: Fight!

Yeah, it'd be suicidally risky, reckless, and insane . . . but his choice was getting absorbed by the Collective—or go down swinging.

Ethan was no quitter. He'd fight.

Shhh, Ethan thought at his wasp. *Don't worry about that hole in your mind or programming or whatever it is. Just wake up. Don't move . . . don't attack. Trust me.*

The wasp's mind woke. It struggled against its instinct to attack the ant lion poised over it. Red primal rage tinged its mind—hot and pulsing and uncontrollable . . . almost.

But the wasp trusted Ethan more than it trusted its own instincts.

It didn't twitch, but its weapons systems activated, the

hydraulics in its limbs silently pressurized . . . and it waited.

Ethan glanced at the fleas, the ant lion, the police in the robotic athletic suits, and the adults.

He and his wasp were surrounded and outgunned.

They'd only have one advantage: *complete* surprise. Because only a moron—or someone beyond totally desperate— would even attempt this.

First, he'd have to get them to drop their guard. Right now, he really wished he'd signed up for drama class when he'd had the chance last semester.

Ethan threw back his head and screamed. "My mind! It's splitting!"

He arched his body against the binding duct tape and straightened his legs, ripping the tape on his knees and ankles.

He toppled backward onto the floor.

Coach Norman and the adults stepped closer. "He's having a seizure! Give him some air!" Coach ordered everyone. He waved off the monster fleas and ant lion.

The insects backed up a few paces.

Ethan looked at his wasp lying on the floor with him . . . into its golden eyes . . . and at himself staring back.

Fight! Ethan thought. *This is our one chance! Fight for your life!*

○ ○ ○ 21 ○ ○ ○

OUT OF THE FRYING PAN

THE WASP JUMPED LIKE AN UNCOILING SPRING, lashed out with its powerful barbed forelimbs, and swept out all six of the ant lion's legs.

The creature tumbled into the air and onto its back.

The impact of the massive insect shattered the gymnasium's hardwood floor and rattled the entire building.

The ant lion's mounted artillery fired with a blast of deafening thunder.

The sound and pressure roiled through Ethan and turned his stomach to jelly and left his head ringing.

The artillery shell hit the wall and exploded, sending steel and plaster and glass showering onto the front yard of the school . . . and leaving more hole than wall in the gym.

The roof creaked and sagged and half fell.

Ethan had expected sudden action, but he was stunned

at how fast the wasp moved and how much destruction occurred in that brief time.

The adults were stunned too . . . but they recovered a lot faster than Ethan had hoped they would.

Coach wheeled on Ethan, his hands outstretched as if he was going to strangle him.

Ethan, still bound in duct tape, promised himself he'd never let Coach touch him again.

Ethan drew his knees to his chest, kicked out and up with all his strength, and connected his heels with the Coach's nose.

Coach Norman fell backward, clutching at a busted, bleeding face.

Meanwhile, the ant lion struggled to right itself. Its six limbs flailed and ripped out boards in the gym's floor for purchase. The artillery mounted on its back clicked as another shell cycled into its firing chamber.

Was it trying to blast itself upright?

"Get it!" Ethan yelled. "Quick!"

The wasp's laser stinger pulled back and aimed at the thing.

But the ant lion's silver armor would reflect that beam. Raw force wouldn't stop it.

Ethan formed a single thought and sent it to the wasp: *STAB.*

The wasp drew back one ripping forelimb and slashed down into the ant lion's belly. With a wrenching shriek, it punctured the ant lion's armor.

The wasp then blasted its laser beam *through* that hole.

The enemy insect bubbled inside, then boiled over and spewed out stinking gray-green ichor over the entire gym.

The two guard fleas jumped away in opposite directions, punching through the walls.

The police officers in exoskeletons rushed the wasp.

The wasp turned and knocked them over like they were toys.

It whirled right and left, unable to decide which of the fleas to chase down and rip apart.

"Here," Ethan cried.

His wasp approached and towered over him, spiky limbs ready to strike.

Ethan felt the insect's heart race. He sensed the raw instinctive pleasure of combat thundering in its mind.

"Get me out of this," Ethan said, and struggled against the binding duct tape. "We'll fight together."

The wasp stared at him . . . and for a moment Ethan saw himself through *its* eyes.

He was small and weak. A mammal. A piece of meat to consume . . . then there was a bond between the two of them . . . Ethan was part of the wasp . . . like (and this last thought was more *his* than the insect's) . . . like he was a little brother to this thing.

The wasp struck down with a forelimb.

It split the duct tape through the center (any closer and it would've ripped Ethan in half).

Ethan pulled off the remains of the tape and stood.

The wasp's cockpit armor slid aside. Interior lights blinked on.

Ethan scrambled inside and instantly felt safe.

He wondered about how easy it was working with the insect. He worried about what Dr. Irving had told him . . . that it was best to be cautious when dealing with human-insect telepathic bonds.

It got easier to understand the wasp, sure, but what price was Ethan paying for that?

Was he becoming less human?

The adults, stunned and knocked down, started getting up.

He and the wasp had run out of time. They had to fight. They had to save themselves . . . and Emma.

Where *was* Emma?

Ethan considered going over to Coach Norman and scaring that information out of him. But Coach wasn't human and wouldn't scare. In fact, Ethan could knock him down and a hundred, a thousand, a million others from the Collective would step up to take his place.

Ethan would have to find Emma on his own.

He and the wasp jumped out of the gymnasium and landed on the brick-paved courtyard of Northside Elementary.

Ethan saw the ruined soccer field, and next to that the freshly overturned lawn of Emerald Park. A half-dozen kids hurried along by adults ran onto the grassy field. They shouted, half panicked. They had good reason after hearing the explosions in the gym.

A zeppelin hovered above the school. Spotlights played over its mirror-Mylar surface.

A second zeppelin was tethered to the field. A stairway had been pushed up to the gondola, and the kids climbed up.

He waved.

That was stupid, because on the cockpit's view screen, he saw the wasp raise a lethal forelimb.

The kids screamed and pointed. Some scattered, some fainted right there on the stairs, and others ran over them into the zeppelin.

How was he going to get them away without scaring them half to death?

A monitor zoomed in and centered on one of the students.

Emma.

She stood, openmouthed, her dark hair half covering her face, staring wide-eyed at him . . . or rather staring at the giant wasp. Her face was contorted with revulsion and terror. Emma was so scared, she froze in place.

Then she did a double take, squinted, fascinated and curious, as if she recognized . . . *something*.

But the vice principal hurried her up the stairs and into the zeppelin.

No way. Ethan wasn't letting them take her away. Not when he was so close!

Ethan would just have to grab her now. She'd be scared out of her mind, but at least she'd still *have* her mind.

He ordered the wasp to unfurl its wings. The exoskeleton casing split open. Its wings popped out and buzzed.

The wasp crouched to get a jumping takeoff—

A rhinoceros beetle landed in front of him. It cratered the courtyard and blocked his path.

It was bone white with orange stripes. It was smaller than Felix's model (although still twice as massive as Ethan's wasp). It had two tiny spikes instead of horns.

Before Ethan could even react, a second beetle landed next to him.

It fired a missile.

Ethan saw a split second of smoke—the wasp instinctively jumped into the air to dodge—but the missile tracked his trajectory.

It hit him. Exploded.

Red-hot needles shot through the wasp, and because of their mental link, it felt like they shot through Ethan, too.

The wasp's armor cracked. One of the middle limbs broke.

The wasp tumbled through the air. It landed in a heap.

Ethan's vision smeared into a blur. He heard the whine of a high-pressure leak. His hands, arms, and legs went numb.

He lay there . . . unable to move . . . or think.

"Ethan? Ethan!"

He had to be dreaming, because that was Madison—screaming in his ear. As usual.

He blinked. The wasp's cockpit came back into focus.

On a fractured view screen Ethan saw two enemy beetles shuffle toward him.

He tried to move. The wasp wouldn't respond.

Three *more* insects landed, their wings a haze that settled into green-and-yellow locust shapes the size of trucks.

There was no way he could fight all these things alone.

He was as good as dead.

° ° ° 22 ° ° °

INTO THE FIRE

A LOCUST POUNCED ONTO ETHAN'S WASP. IT grabbed the wasp's busted leg with jagged forelimbs and razor-edged jaws—and pulled. The wasp's joints wrenched and popped.

It was trying to rip his leg off!

Ethan yanked his arm uselessly within the wasp's limb, desperately urging the fighting suit to move.

Instead of getting *more* scared, though, Ethan felt something turn inside his head . . . and he got mad.

This wasn't a fair fight.

It'd *never* been a fair fight.

Ethan had been set up his entire life to lose. No matter how hard he tried—the grades he got in school, the awards, the soccer matches he won—he was going to grow up and become an adult. He couldn't stop that. He couldn't stop becoming one of the Ch'zar.

Unless he *resisted* them. Unless he *fought*.

The rage he'd felt before in the wasp's mind was back but now was inside *his* brain as well.

He moved. The wasp moved with him.

They slashed at the locust.

The wasp's forelimb caught in the locust's serrated mandibles. They locked, and the two insects struggled.

He pulled at the locust's head. The locust worked its jaws trying to bite through the wasp's arm.

Ethan screamed with rage.

He and his wasp yanked free of the jaws—ripped them out, along with the lower part of the locust's head. Goo and brains squirted over the school's courtyard with a wet *splat*.

He pushed the dead insect off.

Alarms blared inside the cockpit, and red lines and missile icons flashed on-screen.

Ethan instinctively jumped.

Two missiles hit the ground where he'd been standing a split second before.

The wasp landed on the creaking roof of the gymnasium.

The two enemy rhinoceros beetles lumbered toward the smoking crater where he'd been . . . not realizing he'd escaped.

How was he going to stop these guys?

"Blackwood!" Madison's voice crackled through the radio speaker in the cockpit.

"Madison?"

Was it her? He hadn't just dreamed that a second ago?

Ethan wanted to gush his thanks, ask her a million questions—like how she'd found him—but then she'd just tell him what a moron he was.

Instead, Ethan asked, "Where are you?"

"Where are *you*?" she demanded, irritated. "Turn off your stupid stealth mode so we can get a fix on you!"

Ethan glanced about the cockpit. The purple indicators that had lit when he'd gone into stealth mode still glowed. He tapped the nearest button, and they went dark.

"I got you," she whispered. "Hang tight, rookie."

The air filled with buzzing.

Against the lightening star-filled twilight sky, Ethan spied flitting dark shapes.

A dragonfly zoomed overhead—there—gone—then a trailing sonic boom.

He'd never heard a more beautiful sound.

A dozen rhinoceros beetles landed in a V formation. They shook the ground with their massive presence. They were Resisters in midnight blue armor, horns sparking with plasma—and they blasted the enemy beetles and locusts to ashes.

"Felix!" Ethan cried.

"Right here, friend."

A swarm of yellow-and-black-striped Infiltrator wasps engaged enemy red wasps and drones. Lasers and missiles crisscrossed the darkness.

Wounded drones crashed into Main Street.

"You think you get to run off and get all the glory?" Madison demanded.

"Besides," Felix said, "Colonel Winter says we never leave team members behind enemy—"

Madison broke in: "Robot and insect reinforcements inbound. North by northeast. Lots."

Segmented centipede-like earth movers splintered through houses and overturned cars. Wolf spiders bounded across rooftops, smashing chimneys. Roaches boiled up through the sewers, pushing aside the concrete sidewalks like they were tissue paper.

A gigantic tarantula bounded onto the gym's roof and leaped straight at Ethan's wasp.

The wasp jumped out of the way, wings snapped out to fly—and got blindsided by one of the smaller Ch'zar beetles.

The white-and-orange beetle was a clumsy flier but a *fantastic* wrestler as it clutched him with six pronged legs. The beetle's side missile launchers popped open.

It was going to blast him into pieces at point-blank range!

Ethan stopped beating his wasp wings.

Wasp and beetle dropped like two stones—and landed on the crumpled remains of the soccer field.

Ethan shifted his grip, focusing on shutting those missile launcher pods. He pushed the doors halfway closed—enough so they couldn't fire—but hydraulics inside the enemy beetle's shell kicked on and started slowly pushing the pods back open.

Ethan wasn't going to win a contest of brute force with this thing.

He glanced at his monitors (the ones still working) and made sure there were no students on the field. One wrong move and he'd squish his classmates.

Along the corridors and on the grassy fields of Northside Elementary, Resister beetles grappled with mechanical centipedes and spiders and multiarmed robots.

Bombs rained from the air. Streaks of fire shot through the night.

Explosions flattened buildings.

Concrete chunks rained around Ethan's wasp.

The soccer field was thankfully clear of students.

The zeppelin that had been tethered in the adjacent park slowly rose above the battle.

Emma was on that thing!

He had to get out of this beetle's death grip before it was too late.

Ethan watched as the beetle's missile launcher doors continued to push open. Orange-tipped rockets clicked into view. They reminded him of the rockets he and Emma had built, what seemed like a million years ago; only *these* rockets were packed with high explosives.

If fired at this close range, the beetle would blow itself up along with Ethan.

Which was how he had to destroy it.

He curled the wasp's stinger against its abdomen, heated the laser's firing chamber . . . and took *very* careful aim.

He'd get only one shot.

Ethan released his hold and pushed off the beetle.

He ripped free of its grip.

The missile launcher doors immediately popped fully open.

He fired the wasp's laser.

The missiles heated red, then white-hot, and detonated in their launch tubes.

Like a string of firecrackers, all the missiles inside the beetle blew up one after another. The explosions threw Ethan clear of the field and into the wall of the gymnasium, which made the rest of that building collapse.

Ethan's wasp crawled out of the rubble.

The soccer field, crumpled and destroyed before, was now a smoldering, half-molten titanium crater.

The rest of his school was leveled. The classrooms, the chemistry lab, and even the cafeteria had been knocked down and were on fire.

A giant midnight blue rhinoceros beetle landed next to Ethan with a thud. Plasma wisps flickered between its horns.

It had better be friendly . . . because Ethan didn't feel like he had any fight left in him.

Felix's voice came over the radio: "You okay in there? Your suit looks bad."

Inside the cockpit all the indicator lights winked angry red. On the last working monitor he saw that every inch of the wasp's armor had been dented, scratched, punctured, or charred. Ichor and hydraulic fluid leaked from the joints.

"I . . . I think I'm okay. I'm not so sure about my wasp."

My wasp.

Ethan felt every cell in the insect, bruised and battered, as if their bodies were one. He mentally detached himself from the insect . . . while he still could.

"Stand by, Ethan," Felix ordered. "Madison, you're a go to launch your attack."

"Roger that," Madison replied. Her voice was tight with tension and excitement.

Her dragonfly's afterburners flared, and she streaked across the night.

Ethan's view screen zoomed in and highlighted a sleek winged torpedo clutched in her dragonfly's front pincers.

She accelerated straight toward the zeppelin and released the torpedo.

It hit the silver prow of the airship.

Fire blossomed and shot inside, curled and boiled along its length, blew out its sides, and left a flaming aluminum rib cage that rose into the air for a second . . . and then fell to the ground in a smoldering heap.

Ethan felt the fire burning inside him for an instant.

"Emma!" he cried. He started toward the wreckage.

He had to pull her out . . . even if it killed him.

Felix's beetle held him back.

"No, Ethan," he said. "Your sister wasn't on *that* ship. No one was . . . except maybe about a hundred artillery ant lions camouflaged on top."

Ethan slumped to the ground. He was weak. He could literally feel the life seeping out of him.

"Listen to me." Felix gently shook him. "You're leaking hydraulic fluid from your primary reserve. There's a shut-off valve under the main display. Twist it off. Quick!"

Ethan fumbled under the main monitor and found the valve. He twisted it shut.

At once his and the wasp's dizziness cleared.

He and the wasp got up—wobbled, but stayed up.

The other zeppelin turned and rose above the flames.

"We've got to go after them," Ethan said.

"Inbound enemy targets on-screen," Madison reported. "Tracking *three hundred*. We've got to fall back."

"You heard her," Felix whispered. "You tried. We fought, and we won this battle—using *your* plan, Ethan, the one you outlined to Colonel Winter . . . and we did it without losing a single pilot."

Ethan shook his head. He wasn't giving up.

"But if we stay and fight any more," Felix continued, "we'll lose everything, including your sister. You have to come with us. Think, Ethan."

Ethan couldn't answer him.

He *would* do whatever it took to save his sister. He watched the airship as it rose higher and its silver surface glimmered and faded so it looked like a ghost.

Ethan couldn't rescue her while she was on that zeppelin, though. It was too well guarded . . . and far too fragile.

He'd have to find another way.

So had this battle been for nothing? He'd risked his life, Emma's, and those of the Resister pilots who'd come to his rescue. For what?

What had they accomplished?

He looked around. His school and Main Street were in ruins. Fire trucks screamed around the corner. Crowds gathered and watched and pointed.

Those people were adults . . . but there were a few children, too, huddled protectively together. Parents tried to shield their kids, but they couldn't stop them *all* from seeing.

One day Santa Blanca had been normal and perfect— and then tonight their world had been invaded by titanic robots and giant bugs fighting a war in the middle of their neighborhood.

Everyone had seen them.

They'd ask questions.

The Ch'zar couldn't cover it up with convenient lies.

Some of those kids would learn the truth. Some might fight.

One day dozens or hundreds might join the Resisters and win freedom for everyone.

Felix had said something about thinking this through.

And the Ch'zar—through Coach—had themselves taught Ethan: *Superior long-range strategy always wins over superior immediate tactics.*

This might be the key to the strategy he needed—not just for saving Emma or winning any battle, but for the entire war.

"Incoming locust formation at twenty-five miles and closing fast," Madison reported.

Ethan took a last look at the zeppelin. A flicker of reflected fire shone on its silver skin, and then its outline faded into the darkness.

He'd rescue Emma. One day.

But tonight, the strategic and smart thing to do was survive and live to fight tomorrow.

He unfurled his wasp wings and gave them an experimental buzz to see if they still worked. They did, and he rose into the air.

Felix and Madison joined him. A dozen wasps, rhinoceros beetles, and dragonflies gathered in a V formation.

They dropped into stealth mode . . . and became as dark and silent as the night.

∘ ∘ ∘ 23 ∘ ∘ ∘

TREASON

ETHAN GOT PULLED OUT OF THE COCKPIT by four adult technicians in white coveralls. One checked him for serious injuries and tried to make him lie down on a cot. Ethan refused.

The other technicians swarmed over his I.C.E. wasp suit, taping flat caterpillar bandages over its punctures, spraying sealant foam onto the leaking joints, and attaching leads to medical monitors that flashed with erratic vital signs.

On the deck of the hangar, beetle and wasp and dragonfly fighting suits steamed from their still-red-hot jets.

It'd been a long flight, and they'd used up most of their fuel on afterburners to outmaneuver enemy patrols that were everywhere.

The Ch'zar had been desperate to find and destroy them.

Cockpit hatches opened and pilots spilled out of the

suits. Felix, Madison, and the other Resister pilots gathered around Ethan. They all watched the technicians work on his wasp.

Despite the technicians' efforts, the insect curled up into a ball on the hangar floor.

"Will it live?" Felix asked.

A technician shook his head. "We'll know more in a few hours."

Ethan felt sick. He'd messed everything up. If the wasp died because of him . . .

His mind recoiled at the possibility.

He wanted to go over and touch the insect, comfort it somehow, but he knew it had wanted to fight. Ethan sensed satisfaction and pride within the creature. It had battled an enemy force of superior strength and numbers, won, and managed to limp home.

If it died now . . . it would die happy.

Colonel Winter and Dr. Irving and three other adults in military uniforms entered the hangar.

The technicians ignored them and kept working. The pilots snapped to attention.

Ethan stood with the pilots to face the colonel.

Judging by the way she clenched her jaw and looked like she wanted to make good on her threat to march Ethan before a firing squad, he knew this wouldn't end well.

Colonel Winter asked Felix, "All I.C.E.s accounted for, Sergeant?"

"Yes, ma'am," Felix replied.

"Casualties?" the colonel asked.

"We all made it back," Felix replied. "But two pilots and six suits injured . . . one Infiltrator wasp in critical condition."

"Acceptable." She looked over the assembled pilots. "Well fought, all of you."

Her gaze sharpened to a razor-edged glare as she took in Ethan. "I now convene a general court-martial to determine the fate of Mr. Blackwood. Stand to and witness."

The assembled pilots, who'd been at attention before, snapped to an even more rigid, eyes-forward stance.

The strength drained from Ethan and he felt like sitting down, but knew he'd better stay standing. Wasn't a court-martial a military trial of some sort?

He was about to ask, but he saw Felix shake his head slightly.

Even Madison looked scared.

Not one of the other pilots looked at Ethan.

Colonel Winter consulted the tablet computer in her hand. "This military tribunal for a general court-martial is hereby called to order," she said. "Mr. Blackwood is charged with three counts of disobeying orders and disregard of numerous flight regulations, reckless endangerment of military equipment and personnel . . . and *treason*."

Treason? Ethan wanted to protest that he was no traitor—not for the Ch'zar!

He swallowed, though, and kept his mouth shut.

Technically that charge might be true. He *had* endangered the Resistance effort by letting the wasp I.C.E. technology fall into enemy hands.

"How do you plead?" the colonel asked.

There was no denying that he had snuck out and stolen the wasp. It didn't matter *why* he'd done it. It didn't matter that they'd all made it back, either. If Felix and Madison and the other pilots hadn't risked their lives to save his . . . this could have turned out a lot different.

"Guilty, I guess," Ethan whispered.

Felix cleared his throat.

"You have something to say on behalf of the accused, Sergeant?"

"Yes, ma'am," Felix replied. Beads of sweat glistened on his forehead, but his voice never wavered. "The charges are correct—for a pilot in the Resistance. Mr. Blackwood is a civilian, though, and not subject to military regulations. He's not sworn our oath of allegiance. And he was brought in without his consent."

"A technicality," the colonel replied, glaring at Felix. "He never gave us his consent because he was brought in wounded and unconscious and would've *died* without our assistance."

"And yet," Dr. Irving interrupted, "the sergeant's facts are correct. Mr. Blackwood's legal status is undetermined. We can't court-martial a civilian who is neither part of our organization nor the enemy's Collective."

"Are you a lawyer now, Doctor?"

Dr. Irving raised one eyebrow. "I would stand as legal counsel for Mr. Blackwood," he told her, "*should* the need arise."

The two adults stared at each other.

Madison cleared her throat, and when they ignored her, she cleared it again, louder.

"You obviously have an opinion, Corporal," the colonel said without looking at her. "By all means . . ."

Madison stood straighter and said, "Ethan's the most reckless pilot I've ever seen, ma'am, but he also has skills that I've never seen before. No one in a wasp suit takes on an ant lion and wins! And not even I can coax an I.C.E. suit into active stealth for hours at a time! We *need* flyers like him."

Her face burned bright red, but she went on, "Just think what he could do for us if he was *really* trained. Or if some sense got slapped into his thick skull."

"Hey!" Ethan whispered.

Madison glanced at him and mouthed, *"What?"*

"That is enough," the colonel snapped. She looked once more at Dr. Irving, who shrugged back at her. "Very well," she said. "I shall consider the relevant facts."

The colonel nodded at the head technician tending to Ethan's wasp. He tapped a button on the medical monitor. Colonel Winter then consulted her tablet as new data flashed on the screen. "And I shall review Mr. Blackwood's flight record and see his performance for myself."

The colonel motioned at the guards. "Pilots, dismissed,"

she said. "Guards, escort Mr. Blackwood to his quarters. There'll be no further contact between the prisoner and our pilots until his status is determined."

Ethan thought the colonel calling him a prisoner pretty much settled his status.

He looked at Felix and Madison. He nodded his thanks to them . . . and wished he could say more.

They look worried—very worried.

The guards marched Ethan through the hangar and back to his room . . . which he guessed was his cell now, because they locked the door behind him.

∘ ∘ ∘ 24 ∘ ∘ ∘

RESISTER

A HAMBURGER, FRIES, AND A QUART OF MILK were waiting in Ethan's tiny room. He wolfed it all down.

A fresh set of coveralls, socks, underwear, and black boots had been set out for Ethan too.

His old jeans and shirt were ripped, bloody, and covered in insect slime.

Ick.

He shucked them off and kicked them into the corner. He cleaned himself and got into the new clothes. They were warm and soft. The boots had thick gecko-grip soles and fit like a glove.

Ethan sat on the cot and drew his knees to his chest.

How long would it take for the colonel to decide what to do with him? Would she keep him a prisoner in this room forever? Or maybe she'd make him a janitor—hard labor that'd keep him too busy to make trouble ever again.

Next to him on the cot where he'd left it was that leather wristband. It had been Madison's brother's.

Ethan picked it up. He turned it over and examined the electrical resistor bead.

Madison had said it was a symbol for the Resistance . . . a symbol of hope . . . of freedom.

What could a symbol possibly change? Nothing.

Why then did Ethan want more than anything to wear this stupid thing?

He started to slip it on to see how it would look, but he stopped.

Madison's brother, Roger, was supposed to have this. He'd been the *real* pilot of the wasp suit and a leader among the Resisters.

What would the Ch'zar make of his intelligence and skills? Would they use them? Or had they been lost when he'd submerged into the Collective?

Ethan didn't know. And he hoped he never found out, either.

He stared at the bands of color on the resistor and then set it aside.

It wasn't his—even if Madison had given it to him. He didn't deserve it.

He then remembered something that *was* his.

He got up and went through the pockets of his

discarded jeans. He pulled out the letter from his parents and read:

It is our wish that one day we'll all be reunited under the open sky—then we will explain everything.

Right now, that seemed like the *most* unlikely thing in the world.

Maybe his mom and dad had had some plan for him and Emma. They had to know the day would come when they'd grow up and change. His parents had had that secret room, those vaults . . . apparently an escape route, too.

One day he'd find them and they could tell him everything.

If he wasn't marched in front of a firing squad tonight!

And Emma? Where was she now? Vassar Prep High School? A Ch'zar work camp because she'd seen too much? Or someplace *worse*?

He felt a stab of guilt—but that quickly faded.

It wasn't his fault . . . any more than the Earth getting invaded by aliens was his fault, or the neighborhoods set up to raise generations of slaves was his fault.

One thing that had been his fault, though, was running off on his own. He had a lot to learn about the Ch'zar before he fought them again . . . and he had a lot to learn about the Resisters, too.

There was a metallic tap on his door.

Ethan jumped to his feet—surprised—startled—then hopeful. He'd give anything for Felix, or even Madison, to come by to talk to him and give an update on his wasp.

Instead, Dr. Irving opened the door.

He had changed out of his lab coat and wore the same navy blue uniform as Colonel Winter. His long white hair was pulled back into a tight braid.

Ethan hoped he hadn't changed clothes because there was going to be a military trial.

Dr. Irving smiled his crooked smile. "Relax, son," he said. "I don't know any more than you do about what's going to happen. The colonel has called for you"—he brushed his uniform—"and I thought it best to break this out of mothballs and be prepared for anything."

Ethan nodded. "That was kind of you, sir."

"Come." Dr. Irving gestured out to the catwalk. "I'll escort you to the Command and Control Center, or what we here call C and C."

Ethan started to leave, then paused and left his parents' note behind on his cot.

For some reason he didn't want anyone to look at it. It was something just between him and his parents.

For some even *stranger* reason, he grabbed the leather wristband that had belonged to Madison's brother and stuffed it into his pocket.

This time Dr. Irving led Ethan to the right on the catwalk—away from the hangar.

Two guards, who had been standing outside Ethan's

door, were part of the escort too. They had holstered pistols and followed three paces behind Dr. Irving and Ethan.

Ethan nodded at them, but he got nothing back but a cold stare.

The catwalk ended at an elevator door. Dr. Irving pressed his palm to a scanner, and after a moment a two-foot-thick steel door whisked open.

"How is the wasp, sir?" Ethan asked.

Dr. Irving didn't answer. He ushered Ethan onto the elevator. The guards remained outside.

The doors closed and clicked several times.

They flew up so fast that Ethan's stomach felt like it got stuffed into his new boots. There were no lights or indicators, so he had no idea how far up they were going.

"We've stabilized your wasp for now," Dr. Irving finally told him. "We'll know in the next twenty-four hours if it'll live."

"I see . . . ," Ethan whispered.

"What was it like fighting in the suit a third time?" Dr. Irving asked. "I've scanned your flight telemetry." Both his eyebrows raised. "Our pilots train for years before they can achieve that level of control."

Ethan shrugged. "It's like working with anyone else you know . . . just more personal . . . like you're with a friend or a brother."

Dr. Irving nodded, seemingly deep in thought and concerned over this last comment.

"I don't get why it's such a big deal. You must've had

kids from neighborhoods before and trained them as pilots."

"Yes," Dr. Irving said, "we have rescued other neighborhood children. And yes, we've tested them in the fighting suits. But the I.C.E. systems *always* reject them. In some cases the insect mind actually dominated them." He looked away, disturbed. "We've never found one who has made a suitable pilot . . . before you."

The elevator slowed and stopped.

Ethan's ears popped from the pressure difference.

Locks on the other side of the door clicked and clanked open.

"Then why did Madison pick me to fly the suit in the first place?"

"Our pilots were too far away . . . and they would have tried to fly the craft, exert their wills to control it . . . and with that *particular* unit, well, no one but Madison's brother had ever managed the feat. I suspect she hoped you'd be able to activate the I.C.E. system enough for the wasp's autopilot to kick in. In a few cases, we've had that level of response from neighborhood children." He stared into Ethan's eyes. "Or perhaps she saw something different about you."

Different.

Like his parents had been different?

Ethan wondered.

The elevator doors finally opened.

The Command and Control Center was a room the

size of Northside Elementary's gymnasium. Instead of bleachers, it had computer monitors and maps of different parts of the world on the walls that glowed with animated icons.

Dozens of uniformed adults worked at radar stations, terminals with medical readouts streaming across them, and holographic tables showing dotted Earth and lunar orbits. Spotlights illuminated stations here and there; otherwise, lights were dimmed and tinged red.

Everyone seemed busy and didn't give Ethan and Dr. Irving a glance as they stepped off the elevator.

The two armed men by the elevator, though, did indeed notice them. They had a pair of icy, disapproving glares that must be a requirement for the guards here.

"This way," Dr. Irving said.

He guided Ethan between banks of computers and humming generators to a center stage raised above everything else. Monitors flashed with incoming messages. Officers with radio headsets whispered urgent commands and listened to incoming reports.

In one corner Felix and Madison stood. They were wearing gray uniforms and had their hands clasped behind their backs at parade rest.

They brightened when they saw Ethan.

Madison started to speak—but Felix elbowed her. She settled for a tiny wave.

In the middle of this coordinated chaos sat a large table of black glass. On its dark surface was an etched map of the world . . . changed here and there from what Ethan *thought* he knew of geography. North America was missing Florida. Africa had broken up into an archipelago of scattered islands.

Colonel Winter was here, too, pacing. She still had that computer tablet in hand, occasionally glanced at it, and then paced some more.

"Ah, Mr. Blackwood," she said. "Very good."

Everything and everyone else dimmed in Ethan's vision. His heart raced. At this moment, his world contained just him and the colonel.

She was going to tell him what she'd decided. His fate was in her hands.

"Mr. Blackwood, you have run away from battle once—and then rushed headlong *into* a fight against direct orders not one time, but twice! I can only conclude that you're mentally unbalanced . . . or have a death wish."

Ethan opened his mouth to defend himself, but on second thought that was pretty much what had happened (commentary on his mental state aside).

The colonel looked at her tablet computer.

On-screen was the moment when Ethan and the wasp had wrestled away from the white-and-orange beetle and blasted its missiles with a laser at point-blank range.

"On the other hand," she said, tapping her lower lip, "you show more tactical and strategic promise than any other pilot I've ever seen."

"Thank you, ma'am."

She looked him over—*really* looked at him, as if he was another person, not a "problem," for the first time since he'd come back from the fight in Santa Blanca. Her dark gray eyes seemed to drill into him.

"I concede that you came to us under unusual circumstances," she said. "And considering the sudden transition from your neighborhood to this environment . . . I'm going to drop the charges against you." She took in a deep breath. "The decision to join our fight, however, is yours. You'll have to relearn everything you *think* you know from scratch. And most of all, you'll have to learn to take orders."

She tapped the black glass table.

Tiny holographic mountain ranges—the Rockies, the Alps, the Himalayas—sprang up. Blue oceans filled in the spaces between continents. At chest height a swarm of satellites made constellations over the model holographic world.

"Before you say yes or no," the colonel said, "look."

Ethan took a step nearer to the map, and it zoomed in.

There were hundreds of neighborhoods and high school campuses on islands and in isolated mountain valleys. Surrounding them were polluted oceans and wastelands. City-sized Ch'zar factories spread out like cancers and spewed smoke. Huge spiral strip mines made a maze of half the Earth. Spinelike orbital-altitude elevators stood from the equator and reached out past the atmosphere. Spaceships moved from the elevators and farther into the blackness.

"It's not just your sister or neighborhood or even hundreds like them that we fight for, Ethan," she whispered. "It's everyone. Everywhere. The enemy systematically strips our planet of every mineral and resource—every sentient mind. They will consume this world and spread to other star systems . . . and do the same to *every* planet with intelligent life in our galaxy."

It was almost too much for Ethan to take in.

Everything was at stake. The freedom of every human who was alive now—or ever would be—hung in the balance.

Ethan *had* known. Felix and Madison had told him much of this already.

He'd just refused to put together all the pieces . . .

. . . because when he did, he realized the odds weren't even bad . . . they were *impossible.*

There were too many Ch'zar.

How do you fight when you're outnumbered a thousand to one? Let alone win?

The answer came from the Ch'zar themselves . . . what Coach had told him: *Superior long-range strategy always wins over superior immediate tactics.*

To make that winning strategy, though, Ethan had to be smarter than the Ch'zar and their collective intelligence. He had to learn everything he could about them and the Resisters.

Most of all, Ethan had to fight and win . . . because he was no quitter.

"I'm in," he told Colonel Winter. "Teach me how to fight. I'll follow your orders."

"Good." The colonel turned to Felix. "Take Private Blackwood and process him through boot. We'll see how he does and then decide what to do with him."

"Yes, ma'am," Felix said, and a slight smile flickered across the big guy's face.

"Boot?" Ethan whispered.

"Boot camp," Dr. Irving explained, and set a reassuring hand on Ethan's shoulder. "Where you'll receive elementary military and physical-fitness training. I'm sure it will be easy for you."

Something about the way he said "easy" made Ethan think he meant the exact opposite.

Felix and Madison came to escort Ethan. Madison slugged him in the arm, a friendly gesture.

Ethan lingered by the large map, though.

It was all out there—the neighborhoods that had to be saved—the high schools where kids like him and Emma would be absorbed and turned into the enemy—all the Ch'zar factories and military bases—and his mysterious, "different" parents.

Ethan realized that as he stood and thought about it all, he was getting older—more adult every second—and his time to fight aboveground and win this war was growing shorter.

He turned to Felix and Madison.

"We've got to hurry," he told his friends. "We don't have a minute to waste."

° ° ° ACKNOWLEDGMENTS ° ° °

Syne—wife, fellow artist, advisor, soul mate, the person who understands me the best. Where would I be without you?

Richard Curtis—part literary agent and part stage magician. He helped shape this story in so many ways.

The Random House team—smart, dedicated, energetic, and utterly professional:
Diane Landolf
Mallory Loehr
Jim Thomas
Nick Eliopulos
Nicole de las Heras

Special thanks to the talented Jason Chan for the amazing cover!

Extra special thanks to my fans, the best readers in the world, who are kids . . . or, like me, kids at heart.

ERIC NYLUND is a *New York Times* bestselling and World Fantasy Award–nominated author. He is also head writer for Microsoft Game Studios, where he helps create blockbuster video games.

Eric has bachelor's and master's degrees in chemistry. He graduated from the prestigious Clarion West Writers Workshop in 1994. He lives in the Pacific Northwest with his family. You can learn more about Eric and contact him at ericnylund.net.